ALSO BY KRISTEN TRACY

FOR TWEENS

Bessica Lefter Bites Back
The Reinvention of Bessica Lefter
Too Cool for This School

FOR TEENS

Crimes of the Sarahs
Death of a Kleptomaniac
A Field Guide for Heartbreakers
Hung Up
Lost It
Sharks & Boys

FOR KIDS

Camille McPhee Fell Under the Bus

PROJECT (UN)POPULAR: TOTALLY CRUSHED

Kristen Tracy

DELACORTE PRESS

Text copyright © 2017 by Kristen Tracy
Jacket art copyright © 2017 by Lisa Ballard

randomhousekids.com

Educators and librarians, for a variety of teaching tools, visit us at RHTeachersLibrarians.com

Library of Congress Cataloging-in-Publication Data is available upon request.

ISBN 978-0-553-51052-2 (hardcover) — ISBN 978-0-553-51054-6 (ebook)

The text of this book is set in 12-point Filosofia.
Interior design by Heather Kelly

Printed in the United States of America
10 9 8 7 6 5 4 3 2 1
First Edition

To Claudia Rankine,
who, step by step, shows me how it's done

1

Make Me

Drea

Perry!? Why can't I find you on PopRat?! 😈

It was so late. I couldn't even believe my phone was buzzing. Venice I could understand. We were best friends. But Drea Quan? How did she even get my number? And why would she try to send me pops? I ignored her.

Drea

Are you ignoring me? Did you get the note I left in your locker? I'm serious. Can you do for me what you did for Derby?

I looked at my phone again even though I was half-asleep. It was almost midnight. Drea must have been desperate to be bugging me for favors like this.

Drea

> PERRY! I'll do anything you say. Eat weird things.
> Change my hair color. Make me popular!

And even though I really wanted to keep ignoring Drea, I worried she'd keep texting me and I'd never get to sleep. And then tomorrow, sixth grade would feel terrible. So I gave her a helpful answer.

Me

> Don't eat anything weird or change your hair color.
> Derby is still a dweeb. I can't help you. That's not how
> getting popular works

I watched my phone for a few seconds, waiting for it to buzz to life. But it sat beside me on my bed as quiet as a stone. Derby Esposito. Drea Quan. Of course I had a soft heart and wanted to help the geeks. But I really needed to focus on my schoolwork and also build the best yearbook our school had ever seen. I closed my eyes, and Drea and her crazy-terrible smile drifted right out of my thoughts. And so did everything else.

2

Cool?

When Javier Zuniga texted me to meet him beside a tree before school started so we could fix Yearbook, I strongly considered telling him basically what I'd told Drea: "I can't help you." Javier didn't understand what I understood: the popular kids ran Yearbook, and there was no way to fix that.

Last month, when I was a new and eager sixth grader, I'd wrongly believed that as a junior photographer I was powerful enough to help the geeks, the dweebs, and the metal-shop kids. I thought I could have some influence over the under-showered and over–eye shadowed. Maybe redirect the ugly-panted and boring-shirted. Even assist the too-tall, the way-short, and the overly medium. But I had failed. The system hadn't changed. And it never would. I hoped Javier could accept this news when I sprang it on him.

I wasn't too surprised to see Javier standing at the tree before I got there. Being super punctual was a pretty Javier thing.

"Perry," he said, giving me a fist bump. "Thanks for coming."

I figured I wouldn't burst Javier's bubble just yet. I'd break it to him slowly. He was such a nice and hardworking seventh grader. I didn't want to totally crush the guy first thing in the morning.

Javier unzipped his backpack. It looked like an accountant's or banker's backpack, something you'd carry a laptop in, along with massively important folders. It was waterproof and there was a place to lock it. I sure hoped Javier hadn't spent too much time drawing up his plans.

"So do you think you can meet me to take pictures next Saturday?" he asked.

It surprised me that Javier's plans to fix Yearbook would begin on a weekend. "Is there a football game?" I asked. I didn't remember seeing one on the photography schedule.

Javier shook his head. When he smiled at me a small dent appeared in between his eyebrows. But the moment he stopped smiling it disappeared. "It's for the What's Hot section."

It didn't make sense that Javier had brought up the What's Hot section at this exact moment. Because nobody even knew who'd won yet. Those people were going to be announced during last period, right before we got out of school. Sure, the suspense was killing us. But didn't Javier understand that we couldn't start making plans until we had more information about who was hot?

"We should wait until we know who's won," I said. "I mean, I don't even know what Derby does on Saturdays."

I was still a tiny bit hopeful that super-geek Derby Esposito had won the What's Hot section for the sixth graders, even though he was the nerdiest nerd who'd ever tripped down our school's hallway. Since a photo I'd taken of him had gone viral, he'd definitely experienced a bump in visibility.

"Yeah," Javier said, peeling his arms out of his lime-green hoodie and speaking really fast. "Derby didn't win. It's too bad. It's a total bummer. It would have been cool to see the underdog have his moment. But we need to focus on the winners now."

It really surprised me that Javier was being so negative and that he'd called Derby a bummer, a dog, and a loser. He always seemed so nice when he hung out with Eli and Luke in class. Also, it surprised me that Javier was wearing a lime-green shirt underneath his lime-green hoodie. I had this belief that if you wore too much of the same color, you started to resemble a fruit or vegetable. Yellow: a banana. Red: a bell pepper. Orange: an orange. This was way too much lime-green for even a tall person like Javier to pull off.

"I don't know. A ton of people voted for Derby," I argued, trying to ignore the fact that with a hoodie wrapped around his waist, Javier looked exactly like a broadleaf leek. I still wanted to believe the impossible, that a geek could beat the popular kids. Even though my older sister, Piper, had warned me that wasn't how middle school worked. Even though I knew that wasn't how middle school worked.

"I can't tell you how I found out," Javier said. "But I know the winners and the losers. I even know the vote count." He smiled again, and his eyebrow dent grew deeper.

This also really surprised me. That was a lot of information to have before school had even started.

"I need to call Venice," I explained. This was definitely

the kind of information you shared with your best friend the moment you learned it. But Javier stopped me. He literally reached out and put his hand over my finger so I couldn't call her number.

"Wait. I thought we'd keep that between us," Javier said. "That's why I'm telling you beside a tree before school."

I looked at Javier and didn't say anything. It didn't feel like he was trying very hard to fix Yearbook yet. The text he'd sent me before school had been pretty clear.

Javier

> Can you meet me by the tree so we can fix things?

And my text back to him had also been pretty clear.

Me

> Sorry. I don't know how to fix trees

And then his follow-up text had been even clearer.

Javier

> Fix Yearbook

And my response to his follow-up text had been the clearest.

Me

> OK. I hope this works

I tried to remind Javier about his texts. Because I wanted to get to the big plans so I could slowly burst his bubble, and then get to school. "If you're serious about fixing Yearbook, we should try to get Venice involved right away. She's great."

That was when Javier said some pretty alarming things.

"Fix Yearbook?" Javier said. "What does that even mean? We're here to fix the yearbook schedule."

Then he pulled out a spreadsheet with a bunch of dates and times on it.

It was pretty heartbreaking to realize that a text that said "Fix Yearbook" could mean two different things to two different people. Because I thought really it should mean only one thing: Fix Yearbook so the popular kids don't plow over the awesome dreams and crazy-good ideas of everybody else in the class. Really, that text shouldn't have meant anything else.

"Can you hold down this corner?" Javier asked.

And because I'm a nice person who didn't want to watch his plans get swept away in the wind, I kneeled next to him in the grass and pressed my thumb down on a corner.

"I talked to Anya last night," Javier said. "I don't want things to feel weird with her."

I swallowed hard when he mentioned our recently demoted photography editor Anya O'Shea. She was so bossy and unorganized that Ms. Kenny, our faculty advisor, had given Anya's job to Javier. I was pretty sure Anya hated his guts.

"Aren't you worried that Anya hates your guts?" I asked.

He shook his head. "We talked last night. We're all cool."

But that sure didn't sound right. Because Anya was super intense and also mean. "Are you sure you talked to Anya?"

Maybe Javier had accidentally called the wrong person. Anya and Sabrina sounded similar. And so did Sailor. Maybe he'd mistakenly called one of the other sixteen people in Yearbook.

"I know you and Anya have a bumpy history. All that stuff that went down between you at her gym and in the janitor's closet," Javier said. "Do you think you can put that behind you for the sake of Yearbook?"

"What?" I asked. Because I didn't think I had a bumpy history with Anya. I just thought she was probably psycho.

"I really want to focus on the winners," Javier said.

A group of clouds floated over us, making the air feel suddenly cool. Javier stood up, untied his hoodie, and slid it back on. All I could do was shiver. Because hearing that Javier wanted to focus on the winners meant that I'd totally misunderstood what he wanted to do. Javier was just like Anya. He planned to build a yearbook that focused on the popular kids. The system was more powerful than anything I'd come across. I stood up and dusted off my tights. Javier rolled his spreadsheet back up.

"This is very depressing news," I said. "Who won?"

"Fro-yo Unicorn won the hottest frozen yogurt place. Fudgy banana marshmallow fluff won hottest flavor. Hottest pizza topping is fennel sausage—"

I cut him off. Partly because I didn't care, and partly because the results sounded fake.

"There's no way fennel sausage won hottest pizza topping. Pepperoni had to take that one," I said. "Besides, all I really care about is who won for the sixth grade."

"Jessi Whelan," Javier said. The words flew out of his mouth with lightning speed. "Do I think that people voted for her out of sympathy? Sure. Being thrown from a horse and breaking your arm in four places is dramatic. But pity votes count. And she's the winner." He smiled a sympathetic smile and his eyebrow dent came back.

I felt like I'd been kicked in the gut by a donkey.

"Derby got robbed," I said. I was super disappointed.

That was when Javier turned things around and said something unexpected.

"Listen. Do I think the What's Hot section is lame? Absolutely. Do I wish we could scrap the whole thing? Sure. Do the popular kids need another showcase? No. But we can work around it. Okay?"

"What do you mean?" I asked. Javier was starting to give me some hope that maybe our yearbook would still be inclusive even though some lame popular people got voted hot out of pity.

"The What's Hot section is over. Done. Finished. The winners are set in stone. You need to accept that," he said. He sounded so harsh.

I frowned at him.

"Say you accept that," Javier said. "And then I'll tell you how you can help your unpopular friends."

That statement bugged me quite a bit. First, he was being super bossy. Second, most of the people I wanted to help weren't my friends. They were dweebs I'd met in elementary school and felt sorry for, who for some tragic and unknown reason had remained dweebs.

"Say you accept the What's Hot section," Javier commanded.

I took a step back and looked up. The clouds were gone. Above me, an umbrella of branches and green leaves blocked the early-morning sun. Even though the weather was still warm, the very top leaves were beginning to turn red. Fall was coming. Winter would follow. Then spring. And eventually school would be out for summer. Then I'd be a seventh grader. And senior photographer. And then I wouldn't have to accept anything I didn't want to accept underneath a tree. Because I'd be the boss.

I looked Javier right in the eye.

"I accept the What's Hot section for this year," I said.

"Sweet!" he said. "Thanks for being a team player. Okay. Look over this sheet and tell me if I've signed you up for too many Saturdays or after-school days."

He unrolled the sheet again and held it in front of me. I'd never realized how big his hands were. His pinkies were larger than my thumbs.

"You signed me up for multiple Saturdays?" I asked. Because those were days I usually spent with Venice or my family or my cat, Mitten Man.

"We're on the same team, Perry," Javier said. "We're all going to be working a ton to catch up to where we need to be."

I looked over the spreadsheet. My name was everywhere. "Whoa," I said. "That's probably too much work."

Javier rolled it back up and snapped a rubber band around it.

"We'll shoot the hot shots at Fro-yo Unicorn next Saturday. Kill two birds with one stone. You'll take the pictures. And we'll probably get free frozen yogurt."

"As many ounces as I want?" I asked. I'd never gotten as many ounces as I want of anything for free.

"I think so," he said. "I mean, you can't take your own bucket home."

"Right," I said. I thought it was pretty rude he'd even suggest that. He'd never even seen me carry a bucket.

"I'll probably just get a medium." For obvious reasons, I chose not to tell him I planned to shovel on nine or ten toppings.

"So we're set?" Javier said, sliding out of his hoodie again.

"Actually, I think you're forgetting something," I said.

Javier's face looked totally freaked out when I said that. He dropped his hoodie in the grass, ripped off the rubber band, and quickly spread the schedule back out. "Where? When? What's missing?"

"You told me that if I accepted the What's Hot section you'd tell me how to help the unpopular kids," I said.

"Oh yeah," Javier said. "That's easy. You need to hold a clinic."

"A what?" I asked. Because that sounded like I needed to get a doctor and possibly nurses involved.

"Have a photo clinic where you put a list of instructions together on how to take a great-looking portrait. So when we shoot those, all the geeks will look good. They won't get their own section, but they'll look the best they can in their own pictures."

Javier made it sound so easy. There was no way this "clinic" would work.

"It's really hard to change a nerd, Javier," I said. My mind flashed back to Derby. It had taken a lot of time and energy to even get that kid to wear decent pants.

"Don't try to change anybody," Javier said. "Just put a basic list together. Tell them what clothes look good. Encourage them to wear the right amount of makeup. Teach them how to smile naturally. You and Venice could do a demonstration. Nothing crazy."

"I don't even know that dorks would come to that," I said.

"Serve cupcakes," Javier said. He lifted his hand to give me another fist bump. This one felt a bit harder. His knuckle actually stabbed my knuckle.

"And don't forget to act totally surprised for the What's Hot announcements. I don't want anybody to know that we know."

I sighed when Javier told me that. I hated pretending I didn't know things that I actually knew. Because that often led to lying. And I was trying hard not to do that anymore.

"See you in class!" he said.

Then, instead of being a normal person and walking with me to class, Javier scooped up his hoodie and took off running. I guess so he could get a head start on Yearbook. Because that was basically what mattered most to Javier. I stuffed my phone back into my backpack and slowly made my way to school.

I was still about a block from the crosswalk when I saw a giant banana running toward me on the sidewalk.

"Perry!" the banana screamed at me. "Today's the day!"

As soon as the banana spoke I realized it was Derby. For some reason he was wearing a bunch of yellow clothes and a triangle-shaped yellow hat.

"Hi, Derby," I said. And then I didn't know what else to say. Because he looked so happy. And if he knew what I knew, he'd look destroyed and miserable.

"Aren't you going to wish me good luck?" he asked, breathing super hard.

I took a deep breath. "Good luck."

And then Derby Esposito sped off full of hope. Toward the school. Toward his fate. Toward total loserville.

3

Thirty-Seven Tasks

When I walked into Yearbook, Venice and Leo were already there, looking at the updated schedule. This didn't surprise me too much, because their bus driver, Mr. Whitaker, basically drove like a speed demon. I waved at them and they waved back. Then I started walking toward them.

I really didn't want to talk to Leo. I just wanted to have a conversation with my best friend. But since they were holding hands that seemed impossible.

"Have you seen the schedule?" Venice asked me. "We take faculty photos on Monday at lunch."

Wow. Our first free lunch after serving a week's detention and we had to spend it in the faculty lounge working. I mean, I liked taking pictures. But I also liked eating lunch with Venice and talking about my life.

"Nice shoes," Leo said, pointing to my gold-glitter slip-ons. "They match."

What a weird thing to tell me. Of course they did. They

were shoes. But I tried to respond politely. "Leo, all my shoes match. I'm normal."

This made Venice and Leo laugh. Which felt rude. Because I was stating a personal fact.

"He meant they match my shoes," Venice said, twisting her feet, showing off her silver-glitter slip-ons.

"Did you plan that?" Leo asked.

Then I felt bad. Because, in fact, Venice and I had planned that. Because we'd wanted to wear matching outfits for our last day of detention. Nothing too matchy-matchy, because that would be weird. So she'd worn her soft-pink dress and silver-glitter slip-on shoes and I'd worn my bright-mulberry dress over tights with gold-glitter slip-ons. The dresses weren't identical. Mine had much deeper pockets and hers was longer. But wearing them made us feel very close. Like sisters.

When I'd put on my dress this morning I'd totally forgotten about its extra meaning. I was way too distracted about meeting Javier at the tree.

"We totally planned it!" Venice cheered. Then she gave me a quick hug.

"Luke, Eli, Javier, and I never talk about what we're going to wear. I mean, except when we play soccer. If we need to wear pants instead of shorts. If it's cold," Leo said.

It was really hard for me to even pay attention to Leo when he said boring things like this. Venice and I had very interesting lives and always had a million things to tell each other. We rarely talked about the weather.

Leo gestured back to the schedule. "He's going full throttle. Clubs get shot next week. So do teacher portraits. And What's Hot is set for next Saturday."

All three of us stared at the whiteboard. Javier had arrived early to copy the dates from his paper schedule to our class one.

"It's going to be crazy," Venice said.

Then I heard a whooshing sound. Venice must've heard it too, because her face changed. She went from looking just fine to looking annoyed in an instant. I knew what that meant. Anya O'Shea was standing behind me. Because she was such a skunk, it would've made sense that I'd be able to smell Anya whenever she approached. But she smelled totally normal. It was only on the inside that Anya was an odorous person.

"Speaking of crazy," Anya said. "Did you hear who won the What's Hot section?"

Venice kept her back turned toward Anya. "Winners aren't announced until last period." Venice's voice sounded crisp and angry. Which wasn't like Venice's usual voice at all.

"Yeah," Leo said. He loved agreeing with Venice.

"Well," Anya said. "I know who won."

Finally, we all turned around to face Anya. She was smirking and looked totally happy.

"Derby lost," Anya said.

And I wasn't totally surprised that she spat out the news like that.

"None of us should be that surprised. What's Hot focuses on people who are going to matter a ton. Derby barely matters at all."

I could see Venice's face fall in disappointment. Leo put his arm around her and gave her a quick hug.

"You're such a snob," Leo said.

"Whatever," Anya said. "I'm awesome."

Then she turned and walked off to talk to Sailor and Sabrina.

Normally, we would have had a big discussion about how awful Anya was, but instead the bell rang and Ms. Kenny shut the door.

"Class," she said. "We are back on track."

"Woot!" Javier cheered.

"Grab your folders and get to work," Ms. Kenny said. "Javier has given us all a list of daily, weekly, and monthly goals."

Wow. When did he even have time to do that? Didn't Javier believe in sleeping? Didn't he ever watch TV or play video games?

"If you've got any questions about your tasks, please see me or Javier. We're in the clear. Consider our schedule fixed."

We all moved toward the folders and quickly grabbed them.

"Javier gave me twenty-six tasks," Venice said, sounding frightened.

"Don't worry," Leo said. "I'll help you. He only gave me eight."

"Does Javier hate me?" I asked. "He gave me thirty-seven tasks."

"He did not!" Venice groaned, grabbing a peek at my folder.

"Most of them are taking photos and writing captions," I said. "But it feels like a lot."

"That is a lot," Leo said. "But I know Javier doesn't hate you. He thinks you're super talented."

"Don't freak out," Venice said.

But it was hard not to do that.

"Should I talk to Ms. Kenny?" I asked.

"Not yet," Leo said. "Maybe you'll hit a rhythm and you'll knock them out super quick. *Boom. Boom. Boom.*"

I watched as Leo punched the air.

"But what if my tasks hit a rhythm and knock *me* down? *Boom. Boom. Boom.*"

I punched the air much harder.

"Is everything okay over by the whiteboard?" Ms. Kenny asked.

She was looking right at us. It felt like the perfect chance to voice my worry.

"We're fine," Leo said.

"Yeah," Venice added.

And then I sort of felt stuck. Because Ms. Kenny put her head back down and started working at her desk. Things did not feel fine. Things felt hard.

"Look," Venice said. "One of your tasks is to send out emails to the club presidents to arrange photos after school next week. You can knock that out in a few minutes. *Boom.* And thirty-six to go."

"I guess," I said, walking to the computer.

I watched Anya, Sailor, and Sabrina laughing at something at the back of the class. It looked like they were reading a magazine. It looked like they weren't even working on any tasks. I glared at them. I guess Javier noticed. Because he got right in my unhappy face.

"One of their tasks is to put together a list of superlatives, wills, and prophecies," Javier said. "That's what they're working on now."

"Really?" I said. That sounded like a new section. Venice

picked up on that too. Yearbook was way too behind to add a new section.

"What section is that for?" Venice asked.

"Eighth-grade portraits," Javier said. "It gives them a chance to leave their mark."

Laughter erupted again from the trio. Their tasks sounded a million times more fun than mine.

"Is there a question?" Ms. Kenny asked.

I looked at her. I felt myself shaking my head. Which was wrong. Because I did have a question. In fact, I had several. And I should've asked them. Because I deserved some answers.

First: How come everything worked out for Anya and not me?

Second: When was sixth grade going to stop feeling like such hard work?

Third: What was I doing wrong?

4

Piper's List

One lucky thing about my life was that my mom wasn't a ruthless person. She saw what a hard week I'd been having, and she wanted to do something nice for me. On Saturday she let me invite Venice over to spend the night. And she got us pizza. And as a super bonus, Piper came home from college to join us.

"I can't believe I'm putting this garbage in my body," Piper said, delicately biting the pointy tip of her pizza slice. "It's delicious."

It had been months since Piper had ingested any meat or cheese products. But as soon as our mom opened the box lid and released delicious-smelling pizza vapors, Piper declared, "I'm having a slice. I'll go back to being a vegan tomorrow."

Which really surprised me, because I didn't know vegans could take breaks.

"Should I take your quinoa loaf out of the oven?" my mom asked her.

"No," Piper said. "I bet Venice and Perry will love that."

Venice looked really scared by that comment. But she shouldn't have been. Eating quinoa in our house was completely optional. I hardly ever did it.

"I'll go fix a salad," my mom said. "You'll need some vegetables. I don't want the pepperoni to shock your system."

I thought about telling her not to bother, but it was sort of nice to be able to talk openly to Piper without our mom in the same room.

"Well," Piper said. "Not to bring up a sore subject, but I think we need to talk about Derby's loss."

That bummed me out. I'd rather have just eaten pizza and talked about stuff that was going well for me.

"It's a new moon, so I think we should release a wish into the universe for Derby," Piper said.

"Really?" I asked. Because Piper hadn't even met Derby.

"Perry," Piper said, pulling a slim candle out of her bag and setting it in a small glass, "your Derby project really occupied a lot of my headspace. Bobby and I talked about it nonstop."

"You did?" I asked.

Venice sat very politely next to me, and didn't barge in on my conversation with my sister. She was awesome like that.

"Oh yeah," Piper said. She swept a match across a box on the counter until the slender stick bloomed into flame. "Bobby is a philosophy major. So questions about identity and personhood really get his mind turning. Just yesterday he asked me if I thought that the Piper Hall who presently existed would be the same Piper Hall in the future."

"He did?" I asked. Because I didn't even understand why your boyfriend would ask you that question. Of course your girlfriend would be the same person in the future. Unless you broke up with her and got a different one.

"That's deep," Venice said.

"Too deep," I said. I didn't know why it bugged me that Piper and Bobby were talking about Derby, but it did. He was my problem, not theirs.

Piper lit the candle and blew out the match.

"But you knew Derby would lose, right?" Piper said. "I think we all knew that. We hoped he was a boy fueled by a miracle, but really he was just a boy."

Piper was acting a little bit showy. She never used phrases like "fueled by a miracle" or lit skinny candles in our house.

"That's a really lovely way to put it," Venice said.

"Let's focus on the wish," Piper said.

"I didn't even realize you believed in magic," Venice said.

Piper flipped around to look at Venice. "My wishes aren't magic. They're spiritual. I'm not a witch. Bobby and I are secular humanists. We follow a consequentialist ethical system."

"Oh," Venice said.

I didn't know exactly when or how Idaho State University had turned Piper into a humanist vegan who sent wishes out from our kitchen into the world for nerds she'd never met; I just knew it had happened.

"So does one of you want to speak the wish, or should I?" Piper asked.

"Um, you should," I said. Because I didn't think Venice and I understood what was happening.

"For Derby. May you find a path of happiness and walk it toward your dreams. Namaste."

That was a decent wish, but in my mind I was thinking,

Please help the nerds help themselves so we can finally get rid of the system.

Then Piper licked her finger and pinched the flame to extinguish the candle. It sizzled.

"You're deep," Venice said. "I have goose pimples. I think we just did something that might actually help Derby."

"I believe that with my whole being," Piper said. "These candles are great."

But I shook my head. I wasn't totally convinced. "The real problem with Derby was that he didn't want to change," I explained. "I showed him an awesome path to his dreams, but he wanted to keep acting like a nerd and suddenly be treated like a popular person. That's not how life works."

Venice frowned. "He tried to change. He wore different pants for a week, and Leo's jeans really did help me see Derby differently."

I almost stopped breathing. I was really afraid that Venice was going to bring up Derby's butt in front of my family.

"Change is impossible," Piper said. "Nobody can change."

"Well, that's not true," my mom said, arriving with the salad. "My friend Linda went back to school and became a genetics counselor. Before that she was a flight attendant."

"Yeah," Piper said. "But she's still Linda. Her essence is the same. Nobody ever changes."

"Her paycheck tripled and she met a guy at work and they eloped in Bali," my mom said. "That's enough change to float a blimp."

Piper shrugged. "Good for Linda."

Venice was staring at her pizza. Which made me feel bad, because she looked bored. So I decided to try to include her.

"Piper," I said, "we need your help with a Yearbook project."

"That class is so grim," Piper said, plucking off another piece of pepperoni and popping it into her mouth. "You know, you should really consider dropping it and taking up track."

I felt Venice bump me in a panicked way underneath the table.

"Don't worry," I whispered to her. "That's not happening."

"I think we should support Perry, and not encourage her to quit one of her classes," my mom said.

Piper shrugged again. "I guess I value happiness more than you guys."

"It's not a contest," my mom said. "Everybody wants everybody to be happy."

Piper shrugged *again*. "If you say so."

"Okay," I said, trying to stop the fight. "Javier came up with an idea to help the geeks at school, and I think it might work."

"What?" Venice asked. "When were you and Javier talking about a plan for the geeks?"

Oops. I felt bad that I had forgotten to tell her about that.

"Wait," my mom said. "You need to stop this right now. You're not allowed to do this again. Nobody is helping anybody."

"I think it's crazy how we're all throwing that label around. How do you think the geeks would feel if they heard us talking about them like they're barely human?" Piper said.

Piper was so deep.

"Perry," my mother said, "you need to accept people for who they are. Take their pictures. Write their captions. And focus on your other classes."

It really bothered me that my mom was talking in such a stern voice. Luckily, the doorbell rang.

"I wonder who that is," my mom said.

"It's probably our second pizza," Piper said.

"I didn't order a second pizza," my mom said.

Piper pouted. "I did. I'm starving, Mom. I never get to eat like this at college."

"You could've asked," my mom said, grabbing her purse and heading to the door.

"Don't look so deflated," Piper said.

"Mom seems super mad about Yearbook," I said.

"She's just being a good mom. You just barely finished detention from your last geek plan," Piper said. "So tell me your new geek plan."

"Yeah," Venice said grumpily.

"Well," I said, "Javier thought I should hold a photo clinic and teach the dweeby and nerdy kids how to smile and what to wear and stuff, so their portraits all turn out great."

"Are you gonna serve cupcakes to make sure they come?" Piper asked.

I nodded.

"That's not a bad idea. You should hold it during lunch. Write up a list of five things that these kids can do to take a more attractive picture. Five is doable. Anything more than that and you risk them either forgetting what to do or doing the wrong thing or possibly getting offended that you think they all need massive makeovers."

I got out a pen so I could write this advice down. It was excellent.

"When were you and Javier talking about this?" Venice asked. "I sat next to you the whole time in Yearbook."

"Um," I said. Because I'd forgotten that I hadn't told her anything about the tree meeting. "It just came up."

When my mom walked back into the kitchen, I was stunned by what I saw. "Say hello," she said. "It wasn't the pizza you ordered. It was Perry's friend Drea."

There, right in my own kitchen, stood Drea Quan. It was an astonishing turn of events. She hadn't called and asked to come over. She hadn't texted. She'd just appeared on my doorstep and rung my bell.

"Hi," Drea said, unfastening her bicycle helmet. "I was pedaling by, so I thought I'd stop."

"I'm Piper," my sister said, reaching across the table to shake Drea's small hand.

"Does your mother know you're here?" my mom asked.

"She does," Drea said. "We only live four streets away."

Suddenly, I felt really guilty for not knowing how close Drea lived to me.

"Do you want some pizza?" Piper asked. "It's delicious."

I watched Piper take another enormous bite. I wondered if Bobby was somewhere ignoring his quinoa loaf and chowing down on pizza too.

"Okay," Drea said, taking a seat next to Piper on the banquette. "This looks great."

"We'll need more paper towels," my mom said, heading off toward the hall pantry.

"So what brings you here?" Piper asked Drea.

My sister was so direct. I wished I could be more like her.

"I want to be more popular," Drea said.

Wow. Drea was pretty direct too.

"You're cute," Piper said. "You can probably be as popular as you want. It's really just a matter of projecting enough confidence and not being socially weird."

Drea forcefully shook her head. "It's not that easy. I have a terrible smile. And all my friends are really geeky. I'm only friends with kids in the band."

"Why?" Piper asked. "I just don't understand middle school nowadays. I was friends with everybody."

I rolled my eyes at that comment. Sometimes Piper acted like she was too perfect, even if it was true.

"The band kids are nice to me," Drea said. "I'm worried other kids will be mean."

That was a wise move on Drea's part. She'd figured out her clique and was staying in it.

"That's a weird thing to assume," Piper said. "I've never walked into a room and thought anybody would be mean to me. I'm always excited to see who's going to be there. Maybe I'll meet somebody cool. That's what I'm thinking when I walk into a room."

"Yeah," Drea said. "But you're gorgeous."

Piper didn't miss a beat. "We're all gorgeous," she said, flashing a smile.

"No," Drea said. "I'm not gorgeous. And worse than that, I did something really embarrassing on the Internet."

This seemed to catch Piper's attention. She stopped smiling and leaned forward. "How embarrassing? What did you do?"

Drea took a deep breath. "I puked up twenty hot dogs into a bucket."

"Oh my God," Piper said. "Why did you let anybody film that? Did you have the flu or something?"

And then Drea took another deep breath and explained the hot dog eating contest and her initial win, and then the reversal of fortune, when she threw up everything and lost the prize.

"Well," Piper said, "as tough as this sounds, you can't let your entire life be defined by thirty seconds of vomiting. You need to forget your head was ever in that bucket."

And that was pretty wise counsel.

"But the problem is, everybody else needs to forget that my head was in the bucket. That's why I want Perry and Venice to help me. I want to get really awesome pictures in the yearbook, so that when people look back at middle school they remember me that way."

"That's profound," Piper said. "And totally possible."

My mom finally returned with the paper towels.

"Thank you so much!" Drea said. "This gives me hope."

"What are you talking about?" my mom asked. "And why does the kitchen smell like smoke? Is that a burned candle on the table?"

My mom had missed so much. I didn't even know how to explain it.

"Perry and Venice have a super-awesome idea to hold a clinic to teach kids how to pose for their portraits so they look their best," Piper said. "My sister is such a giver."

And it felt great to hear Piper compliment me. When the doorbell rang again, my mom sighed.

"Your dad goes to one denture conference in Omaha and the house turns into Grand Central station," she said.

"Well," Drea said. "I should probably get going."

"Do you want a piece of pizza for the road?" Piper asked.

I was impressed with how persuasive Drea had turned out to be. She'd biked right over to my house unannounced and got exactly what she'd asked for. It was surprising stuff.

"I'm good," Drea said. "But thanks."

Piper stared at Drea in a really intense way.

"I feel a connection with you," Piper said. "Do you have a spirit animal?"

"Um," Drea said. "I have a rabbit."

"That's not it. My totem animal is a dolphin," Piper said, opening up her purse. "Here, take this. I want you to have it."

I watched Piper hand Drea a little white jar.

"What is it?" Drea asked, sounding stunned.

I was stunned too. If my sister had something cool in her purse that she wanted to give away, she should have handed it over to me.

"It's berry lip balm," Piper said. "It's got blue undertones, so it will make your teeth look whiter, and your skin will look more bronze. It's a trick I learned in high school for taking photos after watching a bunch of makeup tutorials online."

"Thanks!" Drea said.

Piper had watched makeup tutorials and not invited me? That disclosure felt very unpleasant.

"Don't worry," Piper said. "I bet Perry and Venice will teach you a metric ton of amazing stuff at the photography clinic."

Drea stared at the white jar in awe and admiration. "Can I give *you* something?" she asked.

"Sure," Piper said.

Drea reached into her back pocket and pulled out what looked like a bottle cap. It was painted pink and white on the inside and had a design on it.

"I made a bunch of these at camp," Drea said. "I sold them. But you can have this one. They have healing flowers on them. This one is a lotus. My number is glued to the back in case you want more."

"Cool," Piper said. "That's super nice of you."

She took the bottle cap and gently set it beside her glass of water. I wasn't very comfortable with what was happening in my kitchen.

"Bye, Drea," Venice said. "See you Monday."

I thought Venice had picked up on my uncomfortable vibes and was trying to help move Drea along.

After she left, we sat and finished our pizza without talking much. I thought it was because my mom was sitting right there.

"She seems really nice," my mom said. "I don't think you've mentioned her before."

And I wanted to explain to my mom that Drea was a geek who needed my help. That having a geek plan wasn't such a bad thing. That sometimes people needed the guidance of other people even if it interfered with homework. But I didn't.

I said, "Yeah. She's in my grade, but I had no idea she lived four streets away."

Piper's phone buzzed to life. I suspected it was Bobby. "If you need more help, just ask," she said, walking into the other room to take the call.

Venice's phone buzzed. "It's Leo," she said. "Do you mind if I take it?"

"No," I said. Because I was trying to be more accepting of my best friend's boyfriend. Even though it was hard.

I looked at my mom. She smiled at me. "We've got each other."

"Yeah," I said. I felt glad about that.

"You know what I was thinking might be fun?" she asked.

I shook my head. "That's okay, Mom. I don't need to do anything fun." Waiting for Piper and Venice to end their calls and return to the table was safer than doing a possibly fun/weird thing with my mom.

"Don't mope, Perry. Listen, I've been thinking that it's time to reestablish the craft corner in the garage. Declutter. Clean off the counters. Maybe start painting pottery again."

I blinked. Why did my mom think I wanted to paint pottery in the garage with her? Whenever I went into the garage I always held my breath, wore shoes so I could stomp on spiders, and left as fast as I could.

"I'm pretty busy with school," I said. "But you could do that."

My mom sighed. "I could do that." She looked down at her hands. Ever since she'd stopped working part-time at my dad's dental practice, she'd been at loose ends. "Do you want more of this or should I wrap it up and put it in the fridge?"

I looked at the pizza all shiny with grease. I didn't feel hungry anymore.

"Wrap it," I said.

So many deep things had happened in the last little bit. I wasn't sure what they all meant. I kept thinking back to Bobby's question to Piper. Would the future Piper be the same as the present Piper? I hadn't taken it seriously when she'd first mentioned it, but it seemed important now. Because maybe the person you were today didn't have to be the person you'd be in the future. Maybe you could be whoever you wanted.

5

Teacher Face

I wasn't actually sure how to get my school to approve a photography clinic. So I decided to take a page from Drea's playbook and be fearless and ask for exactly what I wanted. I wrote up a formal proposal and emailed it to Ms. Kenny.

To: Ms. Kenny
From: Perry Hall
Subject: Looking Good

Dear Ms. Kenny,

Venice and I would like to teach a photography clinic at lunch. Javier suggested this idea. We think giving students a few tips on what to wear and where to put your tongue when you smile would help everybody take the best picture possible. What do you think? Do you have any advice? Can we do this?

But I hadn't heard back from Ms. Kenny in the morning. And I was too shy to bug her about my email during class.

She, Javier, and Eli were at work on something that required lots of stapling. So I refocused my mind on what mattered: teacher portraits. And I kept my focus there during my first four classes.

When the bell rang for lunch, I immediately began looking for Venice. We had to grab equipment and get to the teachers' lounge ASAP.

Unfortunately, instead of crossing paths with Venice when I went into the Yearbook room to retrieve the camera, I bumped into Anya. "I hope you don't screw it up. Teachers are hard. They never look natural." Anya said this while wearing a very intimidating outfit: a tiered, retro-looking lavender tunic, silver jewelry, a white crocodile belt, and superdark jeans. And even though most people would wear shoes that matched a color already in their outfit, Anya had on supershiny green jelly flats. But instead of looking weird, they looked fierce. Just like Anya.

I made myself stop looking at her intense shoes. "I'm sure I'll take awesome portraits," I said, forcing myself to project confidence. "I'm very talented." I was surprised I sounded so smooth and assured. And I think she was too. Because she didn't have a good comeback.

"Whatever," Anya said, walking past me out of the room.

Venice ran up and kissed her hand and then smacked me with it on the cheek. "You slayed her!"

I thought Venice was hilarious. "Anya is such a downer."

"Totally," Venice said. "But I love her shoes."

We speed-walked to the teachers' lounge and when we entered, it felt a little bit like walking into the pet store at the mall that sold exotic parrots. There was a certain excitement in the air and it felt like something unexpected could happen at any moment. Plus, the room had an extra-high ceiling and a plastic sign forbidding nuts.

"Where do you think we should put this chair to reduce shadows and maximize light?" Javier asked.

Was Javier wearing a notched-lapel blazer with brass buttons? He sure was. Where had that thing come from? He hadn't been wearing it first period. I watched Javier drag a folding chair from a dim corner of the room to a spot near the window.

"Do you have a reflector?" I asked. Because that would've been useful if he planned on using the window's light.

"A reflector?" Principal Hunt said. "We've never needed one before."

And when your principal says those words, you stop asking for a reflector.

"Why can't we go outside?" Ms. Pitman asked. "We did that three years ago and everybody looked great. Fresh air. Natural light."

"That's true," Ms. Stott said.

I tried not to feel deflated that Ms. Stott was wearing a shirt with a million yellow polka dots on it. She was such a pale person. I just didn't see that translating well in my lens.

"Would that be okay?" Principal Hunt asked. "Do you mind?"

And I didn't really feel like bossing my teachers around. So I said, "I don't mind."

Javier carried the folding chair outside and Venice followed behind him. He kicked a few pinecones out of the way and set it down on the grass.

"Maybe we should take them next to the tree," Ms. Pitman said. "I love that elm tree."

Of course she loved that elm tree. Ms. Pitman, who was stout in an athletic way, had on a green blouse and brown pants. She resembled that tree. Which didn't surprise me, because the more photographs I took, the more it became clear that people tended to look like the things they loved. Even poodles and milk shakes. You could see it on them.

"The tree is a great idea," Ms. Stott said.

But I wasn't sure that was a great idea. All I wanted was a picture of each of their faces. Putting a giant elm tree in the shot was completely unnecessary.

"Are you going to do a group picture?" Ms. Pitman asked. "You'll need to make sure Ms. Stott is on the front row. She's so short."

"I didn't really dress for a group shot," Ms. Torres said.

Ms. Torres was wearing a cute navy-blue skirt and fuchsia lipstick. I thought she looked better than she'd ever looked at school.

"They are very picky," Javier whispered to me. But I didn't want to agree with that. Because I didn't want to judge my teachers in front of them.

"Ms. Pitman," I said, "do you want to go first?"

"By the tree?" she asked, really excited.

I had no idea why teachers liked trees so much. They never let us hold class outside underneath them. And if you stared at them through the window during class, they asked you to stop doing that and pay attention.

"Okay," I said. I figured I'd just try to crop the tree out.

"Should I pop out around it?" Ms. Pitman asked, lunging around the tree and making a strange face.

"No," I said. "You should stay perfectly still and smile."

But when she did that she looked totally frozen and unnatural. Just like Anya had warned. I didn't want to take a bunch of terrible pictures of my teachers. Javier noticed that too. So did Venice.

"Does she need more lipstick?" Javier asked. "Or less?"

I really wished I'd brought a tube of berry lipstick. Because I noticed Ms. Pitman's teeth could've looked a little whiter.

"Why don't you sit down here," Venice instructed. "And close your eyes. When Perry counts to three you should open your eyes, and you'll get a very natural look."

"Okay," Ms. Pitman said.

Venice was so good at giving instructions. And Ms. Pitman was very good at taking them. She sat down in the folding chair and closed her eyes.

"One, two, three," I said.

Ms. Pitman popped her eyes open and looked amazing. She had a very sincere smile. And her eyes looked kind. I was sure she'd love it.

"Can I see it?" Ms. Pitman asked.

I worried that if I let all the teachers see their pictures they might object to some and I'd have to retake them again and again and I'd run out of time. People can be very critical about how they look in their photos.

"Let her see it," Javier coaxed.

So I did. And to my surprise, she wasn't upset at all.

"That's a great picture," Ms. Pitman said. "I should use that as my profile picture. Can I get a copy?"

And I thought that was a huge compliment.

"Sure," I said.

Next it was Mr. Falconer's turn. I felt really self-conscious taking his photo because he was such a hard teacher. I wanted his picture to be perfect because he always wanted my Idaho History assignments to be perfect.

"Don't you think I should stand like this?" Mr. Falconer asked.

He'd dressed up for the picture and was wearing a gray sport jacket and black slacks. He stood in front of the tree and crossed his arms. He did not make a pleasant face when he did this.

"It would be better if you sat down," I encouraged. "And turn your head this way. Look up. It will make your neck look longer."

"You think I have a short neck?" Mr. Falconer asked.

I didn't think it was a good idea to be criticizing my teachers. Luckily, Venice was right there and she fixed it.

"It's a technique to use when you're wearing a high collar," Venice explained.

"Oh," Mr. Falconer said, angling his head upward.

"And unbutton your jacket," I encouraged. It was bunching up around his stomach in an unnatural and unpleasant way.

His photo looked pretty good too. He came over to inspect it. I showed him the difference between the short-neck look and the long-neck look.

"The second one does look much better," he said. "You're very talented."

"Thanks," I said. I felt myself blush.

"So have you girls picked a topic yet for your oral report? I thought for sure you'd take precious and semiprecious gemstones."

"Um," I said. Because my mind did not need to be thinking about my oral report in Idaho History. My mind still had weeks to think about that.

"We're pretty focused on this," Venice said, pointing to my camera.

Mr. Falconer gave us a quick smile, and then returned to looking serious again. He was the kind of person who never wanted you to know he was having a good time. Which was weird to me.

"Let me know when you decide," he said.

Next up was Ms. Kenny. I knew her picture would be easy, because she was very cute and knew how to pose for shots. Of course she looked adorable in a chiffon-bow top and pleated floral-print skirt.

"She has the best clothes," Venice whispered to me. "How can she afford them?"

And I just shrugged. Because I wished I had more money to be stylish and accessorize more. But I didn't see that happening.

"You guys are doing a great job," Ms. Kenny said.

"Thanks," I said.

And then even though I was nervous about bringing up my email, I did it.

"Um," I said. "I sent you an email last night about having a clinic for the students during lunch."

"Right. Seeing how good you are here, I think that would work. Let me talk to Ms. Hunt about it."

"And we can bring cupcakes," I added, still trying to sell my idea.

"Perry, you have been working so hard in Yearbook. Don't think I haven't noticed. And don't think I'll forget when it comes time to pick next year's senior photographer."

And that kind of blew my mind. I stood there holding my camera and feeling almost dizzy. I started to picture what it would be like when I was senior photographer. I'd set the schedule. Choose the sections. Write the captions. And pick every single photo.

"Hi, Perry." It was a boy's voice. I flipped around. It was Hayes.

I was so surprised to see him at the teacher photo shoot that I didn't even say hello. "What are you doing here, Hayes? I'm working."

"Well," he said. "I know that. But they have coconut balls for dessert in the cafeteria. And I know you like those, so I brought you one."

I didn't even know what to do. Hayes was handing me a coconut ball in front of all the teachers. What was wrong with him?

He held out the flaky white ball for me to take. But all I could do was stare at it.

"Take the ball," Javier said. "We're running behind."

"You take it," I told Javier.

Hayes looked super depressed when I said that. "Oh, sorry. I thought you'd want one."

And then Venice did something very alarming. She butted into my business in an unhelpful way.

"She can't get her fingers sticky when she's using the

camera," she said. "I'll hold it for her. She absolutely *loves* coconut balls."

I didn't want to look like a jerk. And I didn't want to say anything harsh to Venice in front of Hayes. So I just said, "Thanks for the coconut ball."

And then I watched Hayes just sort of wander off back to the sidewalk like he was lost.

"Okay," Javier called, clapping his hands together. "Who's up next?"

Then Drea Quan popped up right in front of me. Where had she come from?

"Hi, Perry," Drea said. "I've been looking all over for you. You're really hard to find at lunch."

"Perry," Javier scolded. "You need to tell your friends you're working and you'll see them later."

I couldn't believe Javier had said that. I mean, Hayes was still in earshot. He could've heard that comment and mistook it to mean I was going to actually call him. Had Javier gone nuts? I wasn't going to do that.

"Drea," I said, "I'm working. I can't talk. I have to get these done before the sun changes position or the teachers get hungry and leave."

"Okay," she said. "I just wanted to thank you for agreeing to help me. All my life I've wanted to be popular. This is going to be so amazing."

And then before I could tell her that I hadn't actually agreed to do that, she zoomed off.

"Should I move the chair over here?" Javier asked, pointing to a weird bush that attracted bees. It was like he didn't understand how the sun or stinging insects operated.

"No," I said. "We need to finish where we started."

Then all the teachers started passing my advice along to the next teacher. "Sit up straight." "Tuck your tongue behind your teeth." "Open your eyes right before she takes the picture." "Berry-colored lip gloss makes your teeth look whiter."

The pictures went quickly after that. Venice was excellent at assisting me. And Javier was a pro at keeping the teachers organized and the line moving. It was moments like this when I remembered why I'd wanted to sign up for Yearbook in the first place. I loved taking pictures. I loved spending time with Venice.

"Anya is going to die when she sees how well these turned out," Venice said. "Everybody looks so good."

"Thanks!" I said.

"Here's your coconut ball," she said, rolling it onto my open hand.

But I didn't eat it. I just stared at it.

"What's wrong?" Venice asked.

"I want Hayes to stop giving me things," I said. "It makes me feel weird."

Venice looked surprised. "He's given you more than one coconut ball?"

I bit into the ball's soft side. It was so sweet.

"He gives me skating tickets," I said. "Didn't I tell you about that?"

"Oh yeah," Venice said. "I forgot."

And I thought that was a rude thing to say, because it meant she wasn't remembering my problems.

"What should I do?" I asked.

"Ask Piper," Venice said. "I think he *really* likes you."

I felt very panicked when Venice told me that. "No! He needs to stop!"

Venice shrugged. "You're totally awesome. It makes sense that he's crushing on you."

That news made me feel even worse.

"It's part of middle school," Venice said. "Remember how Chet liked Winnie last year? And Fletcher liked Hannah? It's just what happens. You should enjoy it."

"But I don't like Hayes," I said. "How can I enjoy it?"

"He's nice. He's giving you things. It's not that bad," Venice said.

"But it makes me feel weird," I reminded her. It was like she'd missed the most important part.

"He'll crush on somebody else soon," Venice said. "I think you should eat your coconut ball, take Leo and me skating with you a couple of times, and stop freaking out."

And even though I thought she was missing the point, I did in fact eat my coconut ball. The lunch bell rang. It was time to go to class. I walked alongside Venice as we made our way back inside.

I wasn't sure she'd given me the best advice. Because I didn't even like to roller-skate or spend time with Leo. And what if Hayes never stopped liking me? What if his crush just went on and on and on? Wasn't there a better way to handle this?

6

Spider Juice

When I got home, I suspected I was all alone. The front door was unlocked, which was helpful. But all the lights were turned off.

"Hello?" I called into the unlit living room. "Hello?"

I hoped my mom would pop out of the kitchen and offer me a muffin or possibly a cheese snack. But instead there was total silence. I walked into the kitchen and opened the refrigerator. Nothing looked good, so I closed the refrigerator and sulked.

When I saw a paper bag on the table I got excited that there might be something delicious inside it. Shockingly, I found Mitten Man asleep in there. I wasn't sure sleeping inside a paper bag was good for the overall health of a cat, so I tried to drag him out. But he didn't like that. He dug his claws deep into the folds at the bag's bottom. Also, he meowed in a sorrowful way.

"You're coming out of there!" I scolded.

But he was not coming out of there. He darted deeper

inside the paper bag, sending them both in a skid off the kitchen table. This made a dramatic thud. So I screamed.

My mom threw open the door to the garage. "What happened?"

But Mitten Man strutted out of the bag like everything was cool, so I decided to ride his vibe.

"Nothing," I said. "Everything's cool."

"Don't scream like that," my mom said. "It sounded like you'd broken something."

I was about to tell my mom not to judge me, but I got distracted by something on her pants.

"What is that?" I said, pointing to dark-gray patches on the thigh area of her light jeans.

She swatted at her legs and giant clouds of dust formed above her knees.

"I'm making real progress on the craft corner," my mom said. "I think I'll be able to unbury your dad's jigsaw too. Remember when he used to make you wooden toys?"

I blinked at her. I remembered getting a splinter once from a block of wood shaped like a whale. And that tiny shard had festered until it oozed pus and I had to go to an urgent care center.

"Those things were dangerous," I said. "I'm not touching anything Dad makes on the jigsaw."

My mom frowned at me. "You're such a downer sometimes."

And that felt like a pretty rude thing to say to somebody who'd been working super hard all day at school to make all her teachers look attractive. I don't think she noticed that she'd hurt my feelings, because instead of apologizing and asking me about my day she said, "Do you want to come help me sort some of your old art in the garage? You and Piper have four huge tubs of it."

I blinked at her again. I was hoping for fresh muffins. Why would I want to go into the garage?

"Um," I said. "I hate the garage."

"Don't worry," she said. "I've already swept all the spiders away and relocated them into the backyard."

My jaw dropped. That was the last place she should've put a bunch of spiders. I loved spending time in the backyard.

"Come on," my mother encouraged. "I want your approval before I throw anything away."

And when she put it that way, when she suggested she might be throwing away precious artwork made by Piper and me, I figured I should go investigate.

When I entered the garage, I tried to breathe through my mouth so I wouldn't smell any garage odors.

"You know," my mom said, "we're lucky to have a two-car garage. Some people only have carports."

But standing in that dustbowl under the gloomy light of two bare bulbs, I sure didn't feel lucky.

"Here we go," my mom said, grunting as she set down four giant plastic tubs.

"Do you want to start with the preschool bin?" she asked.

I didn't care where we started. I just wanted to finish.

"Okay," she said. She popped off the white plastic lid and set it down on the floor.

It was actually pretty exciting looking at my old artwork, because I didn't really remember making it. But my name was written on everything. Flowers made out of crepe paper. Kites made out of ribbons. Landscape drawings accentuated with cotton-ball clouds. I wasn't sure why my mom wanted to get rid of any of it. It made me feel warm and proud just looking at it.

"Oops," my mom said. "This is Piper's. I'm not sure how her stuff got mixed up with yours."

My mother pulled out a photograph of Piper when she was five. I knew she was five because she was wearing a birthday crown on her head with a bright red number five perched on top of it.

"We're sisters," I said. "Of course our stuff will get mixed up."

It bothered me that my mom didn't understand that was what had happened. That because we were naturally so close, of course some of our things would get jumbled.

"I can't believe she was ever that small or wore that many jelly bracelets," my mom said, staring at Piper's portrait.

"I can't believe you were considering tossing these things in the trash," I said. "They're important."

"I'd never throw this away," my mom said, setting it on top of our washing machine. "Let's keep looking for more keepers."

That was when the true horror of what was happening really hit me. If none of the things I was holding were keepers, that meant they were dumpers. Which basically meant all my wonderful art was trash-bound.

"Wait," I said, picking the plastic lid up off the floor. "Let's stop. Piper should be here for this."

I tried putting the lid back on the tub, but I couldn't make it snap shut.

"Piper hasn't looked at this stuff in over a decade. She won't miss any of it," my mom said.

But I didn't believe that. Because Piper was very creative and she might've made a masterpiece or two. I grabbed my cell phone and texted her. I tried to say something that communicated how urgent things were, but without overstating the situation.

Me

MOM WENT CRAZY. THROWING ALL YOUR STUFF OUT

It took three seconds for my mom's phone to ring. She shook it at me. "I hate it when you two gang up on me."

But I didn't think that was what was happening at all. I was just defending my property. I mean, I was an artist. Even if my early work was total crap, shouldn't I be hanging on to it? To appreciate my journey later? I mean, if my own mother couldn't see the logic in this, what was I supposed to do?

"Perry is completely overstating the situation," my mother said. She frowned at me dramatically. "This stuff will eventually grow mold."

I picked up a heavily glittered leprechaun that I'd apparently made in first grade. Of course it wasn't perfect, and I'd glued his googly eyes to his chin, but it just felt wrong to call something I'd spent so much time making garbage. I waved it at my mom. Pieces of glitter fell off and twinkle-floated onto the concrete floor.

"Okay," my mother said into the phone, sounding

exasperated. "You win. I'll wait until you're here before I discard anything."

And it was hard not to gloat and smile ferociously when my mom said that. So I did. But then something evil happened. My mom started snapping her fingers at me. Which felt really hostile. Then she started saying, "Drop that! Drop that!"

But dropping my leprechaun onto the cold and dirty floor felt like the wrong thing to do. So I didn't. Then my mother said something truly horrifying. "There's a giant spider on it."

I froze. *No.* Was she telling me the truth? I scoured his orange face and green pantsuit. But all I saw was my incredibly happy leprechaun. Then the hairy monster moved. A giant black spider crawled across its hat. It was nearly on my hand. I screamed and dropped my artwork. Then I stomped on it repeatedly. Because I didn't want that spider to hunt me down in the house later, which was something I feared spiders liked to do.

"Bye, Piper," my mom said. She slipped her phone into her back pocket and gently touched my arm. "Relax. You've triple-killed it."

But it was hard to relax, because its legs were twitching in a very menacing way.

"Maybe we should take a wildlife appreciation class together," my mom suggested. "Spiders shouldn't cause such a catastrophic response."

I stared down at my heavily stomped leprechaun. I'd torn his hat off his head. It was sad to realize this.

"Or what if we took a hiking class together. Got outdoors and interacted with nature."

"Like butterflies?" I asked in a mopey voice.

"Sure, and caterpillars, and beetles, and bumblebees, and probably spiders," my mom said, giving me a hug.

"I'd rather spend the rest of my life in detention and never eat pie again and have a blister that gets so out of control my foot falls off," I said. And that was a really powerful thing for me to say. Because I worshiped pie.

My mother reached down and picked up my battered sprite. She flicked the dead spider off with her finger, but I could still see a stain of spider juice where I'd crushed it.

"It's ruined now," I said. "It has dead spider fluid on it. And it's brown!" The whole happy green feeling it gave off moments before had been destroyed. Why couldn't we have just left it in the tub?

"We can fix it," my mom said.

But I truly doubted that. Because I'd never heard of any type of detergent that could remove spider juice. I sniffled.

"Until I entered the garage, my day had been going great," I said.

My mom hugged me. "We can cover this spot with more green glitter. You'll never know the difference."

And that seemed like a reasonable solution. Because glitter improved almost everything.

"Do you think we can glue his hat back on and glitter that too?" I asked.

My mother sighed. "It's completely fixable. Why don't we go inside and you can tell me about your great day. I can whip up some muffins."

Finally, it felt like my after-school nightmare was turning into something enjoyable.

"Yeah," I said. "Okay."

I felt my phone buzz. I was hoping Piper was calling so I could brag about all the childhood mementos I'd saved. But it was only a text.

Piper

Next time send pops not texts. K?

That really caught me off guard. Because I didn't even know Piper was on PopRat. When had she done that? I glanced at my mom. I was pretty sure she'd never let me get a PopRat account. Last year, after watching a news show about cell phones and teenagers and juvenile detention centers, she'd forcefully told me that I was never allowed to use any app without her approval, because all those photos and messages (which I hadn't even taken or written or sent yet) would exist forever and destroy my life and haunt me.

I remembered that conversation like it was yesterday. "Is that what you want?" she'd asked, wagging her own cell phone at me like it was a weapon. And because I was a normal fifth grader at the time, of course I'd told her, "Not really."

"Why are you making that face?" my mom asked now. "I thought we'd figured out a way to fix everything."

I glanced down at my leprechaun. Yes. It was salvageable. But I was still leaving my garage with one more problem than I'd had before I entered it: PopRat.

I was smart enough to know this wasn't the time to mention it.

"I just need to eat something," I said.

"Well, I can solve that problem too," my mom said, swinging open the door to the kitchen.

7

Different Legs

Basically, Anya was astonished when she saw how well my pictures turned out. In class the next day, we started blocking out the section. It was like design and layout were going a thousand times faster than when she was in charge.

"I can't believe I'm saying this," Anya said, "but your teacher photos are way more decent than last year's."

It shocked me that she was paying me a compliment.

"She's a rock star," Javier said. "You make my job so easy."

Venice smiled at me.

"Okay," Javier went on. "So where are we on tasks?"

He looked right at me. Which was nuts. Because yesterday I took the most amazing pictures of all the teachers. And today I was making final adjustments for layout.

"Sabrina and Sailor and I have all the wills and prophecies from the eighth graders," Anya said. "It wasn't that hard."

I wanted to roll my eyes at that. There was no way they'd gotten them from every single eighth grader. They'd been working on them for only a few days. It was impossible.

"Wow," Javier said. "You're efficient."

"I know," Anya said. "Sabrina is spell-checking them right now. Some of them are hilarious."

"Cool," Javier said. He looked at me again.

"Have you written up the captions for the boys' volleyball team photos?" Javier asked.

What was wrong with Javier? Of course I hadn't done that.

"I've actually been coordinating with all the club captains to set up photos this week," I said.

"Awesomesauce," Javier said. "Venice, will you help her pick up any slack?"

Venice seemed peeved too. She knew I was being overworked. I sort of wished she would tell Javier to lighten up on me.

"Sure," she said. Ugh. Sometimes she was so agreeable.

"Everyone. Everyone," Ms. Kenny said, flashing the lights to get our attention. "So I need to talk to you about a few pressing things."

The room grew quiet. I heard Javier holding his breath.

"We're making great progress. And for that I think we owe a show of thanks to Javier," she said, clapping her hands enthusiastically.

Javier smiled and fake-bowed. It was really surprising how well Anya was taking all the Javier praise. I mean, he'd basically replaced her and then turned out to be way better. And she was acting totally fine. Maybe she wasn't as backstabby and mean as I'd thought.

"And I also want to tell you that Principal Hunt has decided that for Halloween, the Big Boo carnival will take place in the gymnasium this year. Which will certainly make photography easier. No outdoor shooting. And we might even think about having a photo corner."

"That's a great idea!" Sabrina said. "We can make it spooky!"

Anya nodded enthusiastically at her friend's suggestion. But I didn't even realize Sabrina was a fan of spooky stuff. She mostly wore cute clothes and read gossip magazines and ate vending-machine granola bars. Spooky didn't feel like her flavor.

"And one last thing," Ms. Kenny said, looking right at me. "Venice and Perry have come up with a great idea to do a photography clinic. It will be a chance to learn techniques for taking better pictures."

"They'll teach you how to hold your face and neck and tongue so you'll look your best in your class portraits," Javier said.

He made our clinic sound boring and a little weird. I had one suggestion involving tongue placement. *One.*

"When is it?" Luke asked. "We take portraits next week."

"Um," I said, feeling a little nervous about being in charge of my first clinic. "We'll do it at a lunch later this week."

"Actually," Ms. Kenny said, "Principal Hunt was so impressed with how you handled the faculty portraits that she'd like for you to do your clinic as an assembly."

"A what?" I asked. Because it sounded like she'd said I'd be doing a school assembly.

"Principal Hunt would like you, Venice, and Javier to present your clinic to the whole school. Since portraits are next week, she wants you to give it Friday. Nothing too long or extensive. Just leave us with a few good takeaways."

Venice's eyes were huge. I mean, they were bigger than pancakes.

"Wow," Javier said. "We will crush that."

But I wasn't sure he should've said that. Because that was a lot of work and pressure and it meant I would have to stand up in front of the whole school.

"Are you sure about this?" I asked. I didn't even know how I'd prepare a clinic for the whole school. Wouldn't that require props? Or graphics? Or handouts?

"You'll be great," Ms. Kenny said. "Just do what you did during the faculty photos. Share your tips. Maybe have a volunteer work with you."

"I'll do it," Anya said.

This frightened me. And I could tell it frightened Venice too, because she looked like she was gonna be sick. "Really?" I said.

"This class is pulling together like no other," Ms. Kenny said. "Perry, Venice, Javier, and Anya, you four should use as much class time as you need to get this ready. Pepper me with any questions you have. I'll be glad to help."

But I couldn't even think of a question. I was pretty worried about everything.

"Don't freak out," Venice said.

It was like she could read my mind.

"I've never stood up and talked in front of the whole school before," I said.

But before I could freak out more with Venice, Anya butted into our conversation.

"I don't know exactly what you'll need from me, so just pop or text me about what to wear and stuff. Maybe you could invite a geek up and show the school how not to dress, and then I could be the model everybody should follow. Does that sound good?" Anya said.

Pop with Anya? Never. I'd found the only benefit of being a non-PopRatter. I glared at Javier. If he was in charge, he should put a stop to crazy ideas.

"That's interesting," Javier said. "But I think we only need one example. And then Perry will show the school how that person can look their best."

"Oh," Anya said. "Will I even work for this? Because I'm going to show up already looking good."

She was so full of herself that it was almost impressive. *Almost.*

"Don't sweat the details now," Javier said. "We can work on the presentation later. Let's finish recapping where we are with our tasks."

I sighed heavily. I did not want to recap that.

"Perry," Javier said, "how would you feel if I bumped you up to thirty-eight tasks?"

I thought he was joking, so I laughed it off. But then he stuck his hand out to fist-bump me. Which was the Javier way of making things very official.

"Great. So you'll handle the photography for the Big Boo," he said.

How could I turn down shooting the photos for the Halloween carnival? I couldn't. I stuck out my hand and fist-bumped Javier.

"Venice, you'll help her, right?" Javier asked.

"Of course," Venice said.

I felt her give me a gentle knee nudge under the table. She was trying to let me know everything would be okay. But I needed more than a knee nudge to be convinced of that.

Then Javier went to go talk to Ms. Kenny about something. And Anya peeled off to work with Sailor and Sabrina. I sat next to Venice trying not to flip out.

"It's too much work," I said.

"But you're so good at it," Venice said. "And I'll totally help you."

And just when I thought things couldn't get any worse, Leo walked up.

"The Big Boo is coming!" Leo said. "I love that thing. We should start planning our costumes in case we need to special-order stuff."

That hit me like a ton of bricks. Because he meant that he and Venice should plan a costume together. And that was so rude to say in front of me. Because for the last five years Venice and I had planned our costumes together, because we were best friends. Didn't Leo realize how left out I felt when he said those kinds of things in front of me?

"I don't want to wear anything hot," Venice said. "Last year Perry and I went as Dalmatians, and I basically had to pant half the night to avoid overheating. I really want to avoid fur altogether this year."

That was a stupid thing for her to say. She'd been the one who'd suggested that we go as Dalmatians. I'd wanted to go as cats!

"I want to do something funny," Leo said. "Something that when somebody looks at us they burst out laughing."

And then before I even realized what I was saying, I was giving them suggestions: "Go as two pickles. I'd laugh at you."

Venice winced. "Going as brined food feels wrong."

"But you're on the right track," Leo said. "Pickles are funny."

Leo didn't need to tell me pickles were funny. Everybody already knew that.

"You could go as dirty socks," I said. That actually made me smile. Because that would be a terrible thing to look like for hours at a carnival.

"Maybe we should just think about it more," Venice said. "Do you have any idea what you'll be?"

And it totally broke my heart that she didn't even realize I wanted to plan a costume with her. I mean, I didn't really want Leo involved, but he was her boyfriend. And so I had to accept it. And I thought I was doing a good job. But I didn't understand why she felt it was okay to leave me out of big things.

"You should go as a cat!" Venice said. "It would leave your hands free to take photos."

And I didn't even know what to say. I already knew I could go as a cat. I didn't need her permission.

"I'm going to go as something way cooler than a cat," I said.

"Yeah," Leo said. "Cats have been done to death."

I frowned at him. I still didn't know what Venice saw in him. Sure, I could tolerate him, but I didn't have to like him.

"I actually need to work," I said in a snarky voice. "I've got thirty-eight tasks and picking out your Halloween costume isn't one of them." I stared right at Leo when I said that. And he really got the picture.

"Yeah," Leo said. "That's a lot of tasks. Good luck."

Then he flipped Venice's hair in a playful way and walked off. Which bugged me more than it normally would have. Because when I said I had thirty-eight tasks he didn't even offer to help me with any of them. Which was just like Leo. He never thought about me.

8

Scram Magic

"My life feels like it's over!" Piper said, slamming the refrigerator door shut.

I was so excited that she was home. Maybe she'd have some advice for me. I needed all sorts of questions answered. What should I do for my school assembly photo clinic? How could I get Hayes to crush on somebody else? What should I wear for Halloween? How could I convince Mom to let me get on PopRat?

"I am so glad you're here," I said.

Piper dropped some bread into the toaster and scowled at me. "I hope you're not going to dump all your problems on me. You know, I've got problems too."

Yikes. Now I didn't know how to ask her my questions.

"What's wrong?" I said. Because I really cared about my sister and I didn't want her to feel like her life was ruined.

"First, I feel like a horrible human being. I've eaten meat three times since the pizza," she said. "It's like I'm part were-wolf all of a sudden. Yesterday I ate roast beef!"

"Me too," I said. I wanted her to understand that when it came to meat products and sandwich consumption, she needed to hold herself to a more normal standard.

"Bobby is not cool with this," Piper said. "And it really sucks to disappoint somebody you love."

She sounded so sad. "I'm sorry," I said. "I still love you."

Piper sniffled a little and smiled. "I'm also failing Psychology of Emotion."

I gasped. Piper was an awesome student. That was disastrous news. "Did you miss a bunch of classes?"

"I'm not *failing* failing," Piper said, tearing off a paper towel and blowing her nose. "I'm getting a low C."

I gasped again. That was still pretty bad. She had a scholarship that required her to keep a high GPA. "What happened? Do you have a terrible teacher?"

She reached out across the counter and squeezed my hand. "You are so awesome. You cut right through the crap. Yes. I have a terrible professor. Dr. Weisner. And he hates my response essays. He's stopped giving me credit for them."

"He sounds rotten," I said. Because if you took the time to write an essay, even if it was awful, you deserved some credit.

"We disagree about everything from Maslow's hierarchy of needs to Reiss's theory of sixteen basic desires," Piper groaned. "He thinks he knows everything."

"Teachers are like that," I said. Even though I didn't really think that was a bad thing. Next week, Ms. Stott was going to teach us about the anatomy of a pig's brain. And I knew zero about that topic. So of course she was going to know everything.

"I just wish he was more open-minded," Piper said. "College should be a time when I get to explore ideas. Not have some old dude's opinions about human motivation shoved directly into my brain, right?"

"That sounds right," I said. I was surprised that Piper was this upset over a class. Dr. Weisner must have been the worst college professor ever.

"Sometimes I just want to quit," Piper said.

"Can you take a yoga class instead?" I asked.

Piper shook her head. "I mean quit school altogether."

Yikes. I didn't think our parents would allow that. "But if you quit school, what would you do?" I asked. Because going to college was Piper's life.

"Travel with Bobby," Piper said. "He's thinking about taking a break too."

"Mom and Dad would flip out if you quit school with Bobby," I said. It felt weird but also good to be giving Piper advice, because normally she was the one who gave it to me.

Piper started crying. "Shouldn't I be in school for me? And not because Mom and Dad want me there? I think I'd be much happier in Thailand."

I just stared at Piper when she said that. Because I didn't want her to go to Thailand. I had done a report on Thailand in the fourth grade. And from what I remembered, that place was eight thousand miles away from Idaho and had spitting cobras and deadly centipedes.

My mom walked through the door and saw Piper crying. She set down a bag of groceries and came to her side. "What's wrong, honey?"

And Piper didn't filter her feelings at all. She really told Mom how she felt.

"My life is over! I hate ISU. It feels like a prison. I need a break. Bobby and I want to teach English in Thailand. It's a ten-month program. I'll only need shots for diphtheria and tetanus. But I'll probably get immunized for cholera, typhoid, rabies, and malaria just to be safe."

My mother stared at Piper for two seconds. "No way."

Piper erupted. "I hate Idaho!"

She jumped out of her chair and grabbed her keys. I followed her out of the kitchen. I really, really didn't want Piper to leave this upset. There was a small part of me that worried the next time I heard from my sister would be an email from Bangkok with a photo attachment of her riding atop an elephant.

"Piper, stop!" I said. "Come back. I need to show you something."

My sister turned around to look at me, tears streaming down her face. "What?"

I just stood there staring at her. Because I didn't really have anything to show Piper. I just wanted her to stay.

"The tubs," my mother said with a sigh. "Perry has been incredibly anxious about them."

"Our tub?" Piper asked. "Did you fall in it or something?"

"Um," I said, trying carefully to pick my words so that I could trick Piper into staying as long as possible. "Mom is talking about all our amazing artwork in the garage. They're in a bunch of tubs."

Piper sniffled. She seemed to be calming down. She walked to the sink and ripped off another paper towel and blew her nose again.

"Let's go take a look at them," my mom said.

We followed one another into the garage in a very tense and polite line.

"They're over here," my mom said, switching on the light.

"Wow," Piper said. "You've cleaned off the counter."

"My goal is to clear the craft corner and set up your dad's saw," my mom said, reaching for the tubs.

As she set down the plastic bins, I scoured them for spiders. I also gently kicked them, so that any hiding spiders would scurry out and reveal themselves. None did.

"What are you doing?" Piper asked me. "You're acting weird."

I thought it would be a bad move to complain about anything to Piper, even spiders, so I tried to stay upbeat. "Yeah, I always act weird in the garage."

Piper gave me a confused face.

"This looks like your artwork from elementary school," my mom said, handing Piper a pink piece of construction paper with pictures from magazines glued to it.

"Wow," Piper said. "This stuff is ancient."

"Yeah, but it's ancient in an interesting and amazing way," I said, lamely giving her a thumbs-up.

She turned the pink paper over and squinted.

"What?" I said in a panicked way. I was worried there might be a spider on it.

"It's a poem I wrote," Piper said.

"Ooh," my mother said in an exaggerated happy voice. "Read it out loud."

Piper turned the paper back over. On the front I could see the words *Food I Love Chart*. I didn't realize teachers used to make you create those.

"'I am Piper. I am eight. Here are all the things I ate. Hot dogs. Bacon. Ice cream pies. Sausage. Burgers. Cheesy fries.'"

"Yum!" I said, trying to help my sister rally into a better mood.

"You used to let me eat like a serial killer," Piper said, quickly putting the paper down and giving my mom a death glare. Piper lifted out a red-and-white piece of paper with a leaf on it.

"That's a flag you made of Canada," my mom said. "You always wanted to visit Vancouver in a Winnebago."

"That sounds like a nightmare now," Piper said, glancing at me and then the floor.

When my sister got super negative like this, it felt like she was a different person—a very hostile and annoyed one. As we stood together on the cold concrete floor, I tried to think of something funny to say. Something to turn the mood around. But Piper found something else. It was a bag filled with notes.

"These are my notes from Melanie Soto!"

"Ooh," I said. Because those might be juicy. I wished I had known to look for them. Maybe finding these would help Piper calm down.

"Melanie Soto. She was such a good friend. Until she got all caught up with Greg Nelson," my mom said.

A switch in Piper flipped. I could see it. My sister was far, far away from calming down. "What do you have against Greg? He and Mel are still together. They're a great couple."

"They are?" my mom asked, sounding surprised. "Greg with all the piercings and the vegetable-oil Volkswagen?"

I found a chart Piper had made about running. I tried to hand it to her but she swatted it away.

"What's wrong with piercings? Bobby has piercings. Are you saying there's something wrong with Bobby?" Piper asked.

I held my breath. This was a trap. I really hoped that my mother was smart enough not to say anything bad about Bobby.

"You were a much happier person when you ate meat," my mother said.

I couldn't believe she had said something so blunt and so true. I would have danced around it. Piper gasped.

"The only person making me miserable is Professor Weisner!"

"Who?" my mother asked.

And that was pretty much the end of the end.

"A man I hate! Actually, I hate everything about this semester," Piper said.

I'd never heard her sound this unhappy. Ever. It scared me.

"Don't be like this," I said. I reached out and tried to hug her, but she gently pushed me away and walked out of the garage.

"Stop," she said. "I'm on the verge of a total meltdown."

Wow. Piper had never had one of those. I followed after her, but my mom stayed put.

"And tell your friend I'll call her back tomorrow," Piper said. "I just can't deal with her questions right now."

That didn't make any sense. What friend was she talking about?

"Venice called you?" I asked.

"No. Your geeky friend. The one who dropped by for pizza," Piper said.

"Drea Quan?" I asked. I was stunned.

"Yeah," she said. "She is so insecure. I think she's asked me a hundred questions."

"Wait," I said. "You've been talking to her on the phone?"

I didn't call Piper nearly as much as I wanted because I didn't want to bug her. It was alarming to think Drea was ringing her up any time she pleased. The nerve!

"You don't have to talk to Drea," I said. "You can actually decline all her calls." I walked with her through the house and out the front door.

"I'd never do that to you," Piper said. "I know how important saving the geeks from their geekiness is to you."

But I was starting to care less and less about that. Really, I just wanted to survive my thirty-eight tasks.

"Piper," I said, "can I just ask you one question?"

We'd reached her car, but I wasn't ready to let her go. Piper took her light-gray ISU sweatshirt off and tied it around her hips. "Okay. One. But that's all I have the emotional energy to handle."

So I tried to combine as many of my questions as I could. "What's an easy Halloween costume I could wear that would make a boy I don't like stop crushing on me?"

Piper shrugged. "You can't control another person's feelings. Let the kid have his crush. You should just go as a cat. You like cats. They're easy. And you look super cute with whiskers."

She kissed the top of my head and got in her car. I watched her drive off. I heard the screen door shut behind me and I turned to see my mom. She looked stressed out, which made sense. Her oldest child was considering quitting school and leaving the continent.

"She'll calm down," my mom said. But she sounded a tiny bit uncertain.

"I blame Dr. Weisner," I said. "He sounds terrible."

"I blame Bobby," my mom said. "He's a bad influence."

This surprised me, because even though I knew my mom wasn't thrilled with Bobby, I'd never heard her say anything negative about him before. My mom and I stood on the steps watching cars slowly drive down our street.

"Your dad is going to be late again today," my mom said. "So pick whatever you want for dinner."

My dad had been working so much lately. It felt like half of Idaho Falls was experiencing dental emergencies.

"Does this mean we get pizza again?" I asked.

I felt my mom rest her hand on my shoulder. "I think we should eat something more nutritious."

That *really* surprised me, because any time I ever suggested that we eat pizza my mom always said, "Sounds good."

"Things feel chaotic," she said now. "Let's eat soup."

"If that's what you want," I said, because things did feel chaotic. "Hey, would you mind if I lit a candle?"

My mom sighed heavily. "Last time Piper burned one of those things at dinner, our house smelled like bamboo and frankincense for a week."

"It doesn't have to be a meditation candle," I said. "A birthday candle would work just fine."

I really didn't want to explain to my mom that I needed to send a message to the universe for help. I just wanted to do what Piper had done and get results.

"Sometimes I feel like you and Piper live in a different world from the one I grew up in," my mom said, opening the door. "I never thought about candles or Thailand. I just stayed focused on getting good grades and enjoying myself. I was most happy swimming at the local pool."

I followed my mom inside the house. "Yeah, that sounds like a different world," I said. But really I wasn't paying complete attention anymore.

"Do I have to wait for you to make the soup?" I asked. "Or can I light the candle right now?"

My mother opened the cabinet beside the sink. Inside, there was a neatly stacked row of cupcake decorations, food coloring, and candles. My heart jumped. I mean, I knew it was unlikely that magic was actually going to work, but what if it did?

"Where should I put it?" she asked, pulling a single yellow candle out of the box.

"I'll just hold it," I said.

My mother frowned. "I'm not going to let you hold a lit candle and get hot wax all over your fingers."

"Don't worry," I said. "I'm going to blow it out pretty quickly."

My mother opened up the refrigerator and pulled out a lime. I watched her grab a paring knife and poke the lime's side. Then she stuck the candle inside.

"Cool," I said. It never would've occurred to me to turn a lime into a candlestick.

My mother lit the match and set the candle's small wick on fire. My mind zoomed a million miles a minute to try to figure out my wish. I needed something powerful. Something that would make both Hayes and Drea scram from my life. And a Halloween costume idea. And also I needed help with my photo clinic on Friday. And getting PopRat approval.

"The wax is dripping," my mother said.

I licked my finger and went to snuff out the candle, like Piper had done, but my mom swatted my hand away.

"You can't touch open flames!" she said.

I watched the lime roll onto its side and then tumble into the sink. The candle sizzled and went out when it hit a wet sponge.

"Bummer," I said. Because I wasn't sure if that meant my magic wish would fail.

"Okay," my mother said sternly. "You're not ever allowed to light anything in the house ever again. And if I ever see you try to touch a flaming object from this day forward, you're grounded. That's how people wind up in the burn unit."

It felt pretty terrible that nothing seemed to be working out and that my mom was yelling at me about the burn unit.

"Okay," I said. "I get it."

"Good," she said, giving me a brisk hug. "Now let's open the pantry and try to find some soul-nourishing food."

That seemed pretty impossible, because last time I checked, our pantry was filled mostly with stale Cheez Doodles, Corn Pops, and several cans of low-sodium garbanzo beans. My mom seemed pretty disheartened when she saw the state of our pantry.

"We're living like animals," she said, selecting a can of garbanzo beans.

After trolling through the refrigerator, my mother found a few more ingredients. I helped her make some interesting soup and when my dad finally came home he was still wearing his light-blue dental scrubs and looked totally beat.

"Some days I wish I painted houses," he said. "Because when you're done, you're done. Nobody ever calls you with an emergency."

He sat down at the table and sighed. Work was always this bad when Dr. Pedit, Dad's business partner, took his annual fishing trip to Alaska. My dad had to pick up all the slack.

"Mom made soup," I said.

"That sounds fantastic," he said, slipping off his shoes under the table. "So how's sixth grade treating you? Anything exciting happening?"

And rather than tell him about the exciting stuff, I figured I'd keep things general.

"Things are good," I said.

My mom set down an empty bowl in front of me and ladled in soup. Spiral noodles and interesting vegetables bobbed in the steamy broth.

"Didn't you mention you had an oral report due in Idaho History?" my dad asked. "Aren't you doing it with Venice? Something about mining history in Silver Valley."

I stirred my soup and took a bite. I didn't know why my dad loved talking about homework so much at the dinner table, but it was basically his favorite topic. Probably because he didn't have any.

"That's not due for two weeks," I said. "We haven't even picked our topic yet."

My dad's eyes grew wide. "Well, you should decide right away so you can get started on it."

He tore up a piece of bread and tossed the uneven cubes into his soup. It looked super soggy and disgusting.

"Chill out," I said. "It's important for me to pace myself. I don't even know why you're worried. I always get As."

My dad scooped up the soggy cubes and frowned. "I'm only trying to help. I logged on to TRAC and it doesn't list any assignments due this week in English, Science, or Idaho History."

"That's actually wrong," I said. "I think the teachers are just forgetting to put them online." Because I had plenty of assignments in those classes. I took a big drink of water because the soup was so salty.

"This happened last year," my mom said. "At the beginning everybody is so gung ho for the online calendar. And by mid-November it's only half complete. By February it's worthless."

"It's only October and other than Yearbook I'm mostly ahead with all my assignments," I said. Because I didn't like thinking about November or February until it was actually November or February.

"Both my daughters are such good students," my dad said. "I'm a lucky guy."

My mom looked at me sternly. She did not want me to bring up Piper and Bobby and Thailand. But I wasn't planning on doing that. I was smart enough not to create drama at the dinner table. Besides, everything happening with Piper bummed me out. Also, I had homework to do. I didn't have time to stress out about Piper, Bobby, and Thailand. I needed to stress out about my own life. It was plenty complicated.

9

Shirt Pest

My life was raining problems. And not little tiny problems. Giant awful ones. As soon as I got to school I bumped into Drea. She was wearing so much berry lip gloss that her mouth was turning blue.

"You're wearing too much lip gloss," I told her. "You look like you need oxygen."

"You are so funny!" Drea said. She laughed way too loud and swatted me.

Was she always this annoying? Or was it a new quality? I couldn't tell. But I decided to let her know how I felt about her calling Piper. "Hey," I said. "You need to stop bugging my sister."

"Oh no," Drea said. "Is she still upset? Does she want her sweatshirt back?"

And then I noticed that Drea had a light gray ISU sweatshirt tied around her hips.

"That's Piper's?" I asked. It made no sense that Drea was wearing it.

"I sent a pop to Piper last night about lip gloss. I ran out of hers and clearly I bought the wrong shade." She pointed to her overly purpled lips. "And then she said she was a block away. And my family was making banana splits. So I invited her over. And she was super upset about her psychology teacher. I mean, she was mad at the whole school. And she said she didn't want to be reminded of ISU every second of her life. So she asked me if I wanted her sweatshirt."

This story didn't even sound real. Piper would never go to Drea's for a banana split when she could hang out with me instead.

"No way," I said.

"You mean no way I can keep her sweatshirt?"

And even though I thought Drea was probably making everything up, there was a small piece of me that wondered if she actually was wearing my sister's sweatshirt. If she was, I wanted it back.

"That's what I mean," I said. "You need to give it back to me."

Drea sluggishly untied the sweatshirt and handed it to me. "Does this mean she's not going to give me her other clothes?"

It felt like somebody had hit me in the face. Why would Drea think my sister was giving her more clothes?

"Sorry," I said. "Piper needs all her clothes."

"Even though she's going to Thailand?" Drea asked. "Because she said she wanted to lighten her load."

I felt my face turn hot. *No way. No way. No way was my sister giving her cool clothes to this geek!*

"She changed her mind," I said.

And then I didn't even want to talk to Drea anymore. She was becoming a total pest.

"Okay," Drea said. She handed me Piper's sweatshirt and it smelled just like my sister, plus a little bit like Bobby. It was unbelievable.

"Bye," I said. I tied the shirt around my own waist and stomped off.

When I got to Yearbook, I was really hoping to run into Venice first so I could tell her about all the drama in my life. But I ran into Anya instead. And she looked like a total nut. She had on a fringed black vest and yellow polka-dot pants. I mean, it felt like maybe she was sick with a fever and delirious when she got dressed. And so I tried to ask her about her outfit in a kind way.

"Why are you wearing such weird clothes?" I asked.

Anya smiled at me in a snarky way. "Aren't we working on the photo-clinic assembly presentation today?"

"Yeah," I said. I didn't know why that mattered.

"So I decided to show up looking like a full-on geek, so that you and Venice can de-geek me for the school. Like a step-by-step on how to look like a normal and attractive person."

I just stared at her. I couldn't believe that she thought my photo clinic was going to be all about her. When Venice walked in, I could tell the exact moment she noticed what Anya was wearing, because she did a hilarious double take.

"I'm dressed like a nerd on purpose," Anya explained to Venice. "I figure I'll show up looking like a dork and then you guys will de-dork me for the assembly."

Venice blinked several times. "Are you going to wear that all day?"

Anya's eyes grew wide. "I'm not crazy! Of course not. My real clothes are in my cubby."

I looked at Venice and I really hoped she could read my mind. Because I had no desire to let Anya steal my assembly presentation.

"I think it's offensive to geeks to take this approach," Venice said.

"Totally," I said. Even though I was sort of down on geeks at the moment. Considering one of them was trying to steal my sister's clothes.

"Dorks don't care if you make fun of them," Anya said. "It's like their feelings are made of rubber. Nothing sticks to them."

"Um, yeah," I said, "that's not true."

"And how would you know? Are you a dork?" Anya asked.

And while I didn't think I was a dork, I did think I could understand how they felt.

"We should use a regular student for the assembly," I said.

"Exactly. What you're trying to do feels very strange," Venice said, pointing to Anya's pants.

"I totally disagree," Anya said. "I think I'll do great. So do Sailor and Sabrina."

"Yeah. Your friends will always think you're great. That's their job," I said. I winked at Venice.

Ring.

Venice leaned in and whispered to me, "I'm going to run up and ask Ms. Kenny if we can do it our way, and use a regular student, okay?"

My best friend was so smart. Of course we should cut Anya

off at the knees before she had a chance to worm her way into our clinic.

"Do it!" I said.

"Do what?" Anya asked.

When Venice ran off I had to keep Anya busy.

"So where did you get those pants?" I asked.

"Park City," Anya said. "At the outlet mall. I wore them for Halloween for a bumblebee costume."

And just like that Venice was back.

"So Ms. Kenny likes the idea of using Drea Quan as a volunteer for the assembly," Venice said.

My stomach flipped and flipped again. I thought Venice and I were on the same page. How was it possible that my own best friend had accidentally sabotaged me? Seriously, how? I gave Venice a stern look, but she didn't seem to notice.

"Why are you two compelled to throw all your free time away assisting hard-core geeks?" Anya blurted out. "It doesn't make sense."

I watched her storm off to find Sailor and Sabrina.

"You can thank me later," Venice said.

But I didn't feel like thanking her. I felt like explaining how I felt about Drea Quan. "I am getting really sick of Drea."

"You are?" Venice asked. "Why? I thought you wanted to help her. She's trying so hard to improve her social status."

And even though I wanted to tell Venice all about how Drea was hogging Piper's free time, I wasn't sure how to phrase it. Because if Piper wanted to help Drea and talk to her, that really wasn't anything I could control.

"I just think Drea might be hard to work with," I said.

"She'll do everything we say," Venice said.

And then before I could complain more about Drea, Leo showed up. "Hey, girls. What's up?"

He was always interrupting important talks I was having with Venice.

"We're planning the photo clinic," Venice said.

"Cool," Leo said. "I bet you guys are gonna kill that."

But I didn't need Leo's input. I needed him to leave so I could finish talking to Venice about personal stuff.

"I want to show you something," Leo said.

I rolled my eyes.

"It's our future Halloween costume," he said, unfolding a glossy page from a magazine.

I looked at the photo but it didn't make sense. A fur-covered person was standing next to a man in a yellow hat.

"This is hilarious," Venice said. "Curious George!"

After she said that, on one level the picture made more sense. But on another level, I was super surprised that Leo was lame enough to suggest dressing up as a monkey from a baby book.

"You can be George and I'll be the Man with the Yellow Hat," Leo said with a giant smile.

"That's brilliant!" Venice said. And then she gave him a super-enthusiastic hug.

That idea was far from brilliant. "But that means you'll have to wear fur."

"Yeah," Venice said. "Monkeys are pretty furry."

"No," I said. "The other day you said that fur makes you hot. You said you didn't want to wear a fur costume."

I watched Leo's smile fade.

"I can keep looking," he said. "Perry is right. You said you didn't want fur."

Then Venice did the most annoying thing ever. She grabbed Leo's hand and squeezed it. "But I love this idea! As long as I don't wear thick fur I'm sure I'll be fine."

That didn't make any sense. Because the fur we'd used last year for our Dalmatian costumes had been pretty thin.

"Have you thought about your costume?" Leo asked me.

And that felt like a rude way to point out that they didn't want me to dress up like somebody from *Curious George*. Like he wanted to make sure I wasn't planning on being part of their costume.

"I'm still floating ideas," I said.

"Perry always has awesome costumes," Venice said. "Three years ago she went as a sponge, and it was the funniest thing I've ever seen. She even *smelled* like a sponge."

And it made me feel a little bit sad when she brought up my sponge costume. Because Venice and I had made those costumes together. She'd gone as a purple starfish. We'd looked amazing. We'd plodded through the neighborhood getting candy, each filling an entire pillowcase. And at the end of the night, Venice had slept over at my house. And we'd talked about the costume we wanted to be the next year: candy bars. And we'd talked about the costume we'd wanted to be the year after that: Dalmatians. And we'd talked and talked and talked until my dad came into the room and said, "The talking has to stop or I'm separating you two."

But this Halloween wasn't going to be anything like that. This Halloween was going to be a completely different and possibly lonely story. Venice and Leo planned to stick together like glue, while I'd be by myself. And my sister, Piper, might be packing a suitcase.

"So what do we have for the presentation so far?" Javier asked.

I just stared at him. Where had he even come from? It was like he popped out of nowhere all the time and expected me to do everything.

"Ms. Kenny approved Drea as our volunteer for the photo-clinic assembly," Venice said.

"Drea," Javier said. "That's an interesting choice."

"I agree," I said.

"I really like how you guys don't take the easy road. So many people would've picked one of their own friends who wasn't that bad off. But you've chosen somebody you can actually help. Sweet."

"Truth be told, she's really very nice," Venice said.

"She's okay," I corrected.

Venice shot me a concerned face, but I ignored it.

"Get me an outline of the presentation by the end of class," Javier said. "Cool?"

"Aren't you going to help us?" I asked. He was the senior photography editor. This was his presentation too.

"I totally trust you, Perry," he said.

And then he grabbed the hall pass and fled the room.

"He must have something important to do," Venice said.

"It had better be a bathroom emergency and he'd better come right back," I said. "Because *this* is really important."

"Okay. As important as this is, we should also probably talk about our Idaho History report," Venice said. "How would you feel doing a report about trout?"

I exhaled dramatically and made a lip fart. "Hate trout."

"Well, we should pick something," Venice said.

"Well, we don't need to do it this instant," I said.

"Don't snap at me," Venice said. "We're in the same boat."

But that wasn't true. Because even though we didn't have a topic, Venice was in a boat with her boyfriend. And I was in a boat all by myself.

10

So Weird

My thirty-eight tasks weighed on me like a sack of hammers. When it came time to shoot the class clubs, I felt a little relieved. I could check off one more task. How would it feel to have zero tasks in my life? I couldn't remember my life before I had tasks. How had I spent all my free time? Did I nap more? Watch TV? Play with Mitten Man? Run around outside? It seemed impossible that such a time had ever existed.

We were supposed to meet outside the Yearbook room. But as I waited by the door, Javier, Venice, and Anya never came. I stared at a bunch of colorful posters hanging on the wall. The *Wizard of Oz* tryouts were coming up. I just couldn't picture any of my classmates believably playing Dorothy, a Tin Man, or a Good Witch. And what about Toto? Would our school even let Derby's play have a real dog in it?

I looked down the hall again. Javier, Venice, and Anya still weren't anywhere. I worried that maybe I'd gotten the room wrong, and was supposed to meet everybody outside the drama room. I looked down the hallway. Someone was coming. But it wasn't anybody I wanted to see. It was Hayes.

I tried to act like I hadn't seen him, but that was hard to do because we were the only two people standing in the hallway, and for some crazy reason he was wearing an orange T-shirt with the word PERSEVERE spelled out in big block letters. I leaned back against the wall and tried to send him stay-away vibes. But he was smiling huge. And he was carrying something. I hoped it wasn't for me.

"I brought you something," Hayes said, holding out a napkin.

I couldn't believe it. It was another coconut ball. I didn't even think they'd served those at lunch today. How old was that thing? Where had he gotten it? When was this crush going to pass?

"Don't you want it?" Hayes asked.

All I could do was stare at it. We both stood there in silence looking at the lopsided white ball.

"Hi, Hayes," Venice said as she walked up to us. "Yum. Another coconut ball. Perry, it's your lucky day."

I shot Venice a frown. It was definitely not my lucky day. Why would she say such a thing?

Javier was with her. "Wow," he said. "Is that another coconut ball? You must be addicted to those suckers."

I almost started to shake. It was one thing to have somebody crushing on me who I didn't even like. It was another thing to feel pressured into accepting coconut balls from him.

"Aren't you going to take it?" Hayes asked.

And then, just like before, Venice took it. "Maybe we can share it. We'll need the sugar to get through these shoots."

Hayes looked at me, but I avoided making eye contact with him and kept my gaze on his bright shirt. It felt rude not to thank him for the treat. So I caved. "Thanks, Hayes. The sugar will be helpful."

He slowly started to back up. "Right," he said. Then he flipped around and was gone.

"Wow," Javier said. "Did he do something to make you stop liking him?"

What a terrible thing to say to me. Why was Javier blaming me for how Hayes felt?

"I don't think I did anything," I said.

"Why can't you just take his coconut balls and thank him?" Venice said. "That's the nice thing to do."

I didn't even know whose side my friend was on anymore. "I don't want to talk about this in front of Javier."

"That's cool," Javier said. "I get it. I don't like talking about my girlfriend with you guys either."

Javier had a girlfriend? Wait. Javier thought Hayes was my boyfriend? That was completely nuts.

"Hayes isn't my boyfriend!" I said. "I don't even like him."

"Breakups happen," Javier said. "I'm not judging you."

I looked at Venice pleadingly to help me explain things. But she was on her phone.

"Venice!" I snapped.

"Hold on," Venice said. "Leo popped me something important."

And then it was like I didn't even want to look at Venice anymore. She PopRatted with Leo? When had she started doing that? I felt so out of the loop. And I'd never felt that way about Venice before. We'd been best friends since forever.

Our loops were basically connected. But there was no way to talk about any of this in the hallway with Javier on the way to take photos.

"Let's get to drama club," Javier said. "We can talk about your boyfriend later."

Venice handed me the coconut ball and it smelled delicious. It really bugged me that Hayes gave me such sweet and tasty snacks. I couldn't help but eat it in one bite.

Walking into the drama club felt a little unreal. Lots of the members were wearing face paint, so they looked like ferocious animals. This was how they wanted to be remembered for the rest of their lives in their yearbook? So weird.

"Wow," Javier said. "Rocky DeBoom makes a great lion."

Rocky DeBoom was a member of drama club? When had that happened? I glanced at Venice, but she was busy sending more pops to Leo.

"Tell us what you want, and we'll give it to you," Derby said.

Surprisingly, Derby did not look like a crazy nerd. He was wearing a pin-striped blue chambray jacket and dark jeans. I didn't even know Derby owned those kinds of clothes.

"Nice outfit," Javier said. "You look corporate."

Derby smiled. "I wanted to look like the official leader."

"Okay," Javier said. "Give them instructions."

Nobody said or did anything. It was just a bunch of silence.

"Perry," Javier said, "give Derby instructions."

"Oh," I said. I'd forgotten I was in charge of everything. "I need tall people against the back wall. Shorter people, please kneel in front."

There were twenty people lined up in front of the calendar

of events on the wall. When had drama club gotten this big? When school started, a lot of people thought Derby was a total zero. Of course, I hadn't thought that. Everybody is something. Nobody is a total zero. But then Derby got chosen to be the director of the school play. And then he came really close to winning the What's Hot contest for sixth graders. And now he was wearing leadership clothes. So much had changed for him. I wondered if he could feel the changes deep down, if he could sense his inner dweeb shrinking.

I glanced at the wall of drama kids trying to organize themselves by height.

"Penny Moffett, you are not a tall person," I said. "You need to kneel in front."

It was surprising to me that people didn't know which category they belonged in. I was a short person. Venice was a tall person. Javier was a tall person. It was really very simple. I watched Derby kneel down in front. That didn't seem right. He was the most important person. He didn't belong on the floor.

"Derby," I said, "you should stand next to everybody."

"But I'm a short person," he said.

It was cute how Derby didn't understand that the leader needed to stand next to his group.

"Can you stand next to the silver person?" I asked him.

I didn't know why somebody had painted her face silver for a picture, but she had.

"That's Sasha York," Derby said.

Wow. Face and neck makeup can really transform a person. She looked way more like a robot than Sasha.

"Everybody smile," I said.

And then people made very exaggerated smiles that didn't look good. I pulled the camera away from my eye.

"Please don't bunch up your face. And please don't reveal your gums. That's not attractive," I explained. "Let's try it again. Keep your tongue pressed against the back of your teeth. That will help you guys not be so gummy."

It was a little better, but not much. Why did the geekiest club have to look so geeky? It was a bummer.

"Do you need some berry lip gloss?" a voice asked behind me. I turned around. It was Drea. Ugh. Why was she here?

"I need some lip gloss!" a girl wearing a straw wig said.

And I didn't want to deny her any lip gloss, because she really did need it. Drea rushed over and pulled out the wand.

I looked at Venice. "Did you ask Drea to come?"

"No," Venice said. "Why would I do that?"

And that was the right answer.

"I did," Javier said. "I thought it would be helpful for her."

That was when it hit me that Javier was a terrible leader, because he was making my tasks more numerous and difficult and he also wasn't much fun to be around.

Drea hurried back over to us. "How do they look now?"

She'd spread it on very thick, and it gave some of the paler girls zombie faces. I sighed.

"That's way too purple," I said.

"Did I put it on too dark?" Drea asked.

"Maybe a little," Javier said.

Which was the most useful thing that had come out of Javier's mouth since September. Venice found some paper towels and we sent them around the room so the girls could do some blotting.

"This shoot is eating a ton of time," Javier said. "Math club expected us five minutes ago."

"Calm down about the schedule," I said. "Good pictures take more than an instant to make."

"She's right," Venice said.

"Okay," I said. "I need all of you to smile. And don't try to smile huge. Just a light smile. And try to smile with your eyes, too."

Lots of squinting started to happen.

"Stop the eye-smiling," I said.

"Are all the shots going to take this long?" Javier asked. "The teachers were much easier."

I lowered the camera and looked at him. "You are not being helpful."

That was when Venice took over. She shut her phone down and dove in front of me. "Okay," she said. "Look at me. I'm going to stand next to Perry on this desk and do three funny things. Please feel free to smile."

"I don't think we should stand on the furniture," Javier said.

"Oh, we do that all the time," Derby said.

I wasn't sure exactly what Venice was doing beside me. But it must have been incredibly funny. Because all the faces I saw through the viewfinder looked like they were on the verge of laughter.

Click.

"And we're done!" I cheered.

Venice hopped down off the desk and gave me a quick hug.

"Let's roll," Javier said. "We've got six more clubs to shoot."

It was a bummer that Javier didn't let us enjoy one second of what it felt like to finish something.

"Can I see the picture?" Drea asked, leaning in over my shoulder.

"We don't have time," Javier said. "We need to move."

And in that moment, I really appreciated Javier's annoying work ethic.

As we walked down the hall to the math room, I tried to ignore the fact that Drea was still with us. But it was hard.

"The school feels so dead when everybody leaves, doesn't it?" Drea asked. "The halls feel extra echoey. Listen."

We all listened as Drea scooted her sneakers across the floor making monstrous squeaking noises.

"Stop that," I said. "You're killing me."

"Okay," Drea said, rushing up to walk next to Venice.

It really surprised me how much I could dislike Drea in a matter of hours. Yesterday, I hadn't minded helping her out. Today, I wanted her to disappear.

"Where did you learn to act like a monkey?" Drea asked. "I've spent a lot of time watching black howler monkeys at the zoo. And the way you pretended to eat leaves was pretty spot-on."

I kept walking. I really hated thinking that Venice was already rehearsing a routine for her Halloween costume. That probably meant she and Leo had been working on something together. Because that was what Venice and I used to do. We'd figure out a little dance. Or, like last year, we rehearsed some cute Dalmatian moves.

"I have to agree," Javier said. "You've got great monkey energy."

Venice laughed. "Thanks. Leo and I have been practicing our Big Boo costume."

That made me fume inside.

"Is that somebody's phone?" Javier asked.

Ugh. Couldn't Leo leave Venice alone for longer than five minutes?

"It's not me," Venice said, patting her pocket.

"Oh my gosh!" Drea said. "I've got to take this. It's Piper!"

Hearing those words totally crushed me. I quickly looked at my own phone. Piper had not tried to call or text me. Nobody had. I watched as Drea ran down the hallway, plugging one ear with a finger and chatting away.

"Did she mean *Piper* Piper?" Venice asked. "That's so nice that she's helping her."

But it was like Venice was missing the real problem here. I didn't want Piper to help Drea. That made me feel weird. *I* was Piper's sister, and ever since she'd gone away to school I'd really missed her. If she had time to spend on the phone helping somebody navigate middle school, that call should go to me.

"Drea feels like a sister stalker," I whispered to Venice.

But she didn't totally hear me.

"She *is* a loud talker," Venice said. "I'll chat with her about that."

"You are so brilliant!" Drea boomed into her phone.

The hair on my arms stood up. I was so upset by what was happening in this hallway that my whole body felt electric and annoyed. I texted Piper to let her know.

I kept walking. The plans to help Drea had gotten off track. She shouldn't be having a better life than I had. We were just supposed to make the school forget she'd thrown up into a bucket. And that was all I wanted to do for her. I'd give her a good picture for the yearbook and be done with her. The sooner Drea Quan wasn't a part of my life, the better I would feel about everything.

11

Face Facts

We weren't as prepared for the assembly as we needed to be. Venice had brought five suggestions for smiling. I had brought five suggestions for head, neck, and shoulder placement. Javier had brought a clipboard. And Anya had brought herself. Of course I'd sent Javier an outline of our presentation. And of course Javier had forwarded it to Ms. Kenny and neglected to mention I'd done 100 percent of it.

OUTLINE FOR PRESENTATION

1. Introduce ourselves.
2. Show photos of awkward smiling.
3. Explain how your face works.
4. Demonstrate how to smile like a normal person.
5. Show how body position enhances your overall look.

Drea met us in the Yearbook room. She was dressed super cute in a spearmint-colored T-shirt, jean skirt, and gray ankle boots. She also looked very eager.

"This is the most exciting thing I've ever done," Drea said, twisting nervously in her boots.

That was sort of surprising, because I thought being in band and marching in parades had to be somewhat exciting.

"Let's just make sure we follow the outline," Javier said. "To simplify things, I'll introduce everybody."

Anya released a disgusted sound. "I could do that."

"You could," Javier said. "But I'm the one in charge and I just said that I'm doing it."

Even though Javier was crushing me with tasks, I really appreciated his leadership abilities when it came to Anya. He didn't pull punches.

"Here's what I'm going to say about smiling," Venice said, handing Javier her script.

He looked it over and nodded. "These are great."

"Here's what I'm going to say." I handed Javier a rough outline.

"I expected more detail from you," Javier said.

"Me too," Anya said, glancing over my shoulder.

"You guys ready to head down to the gymnasium?" Ms. Kenny asked.

We all said we were. As we walked down the hallway, Drea kept hopping up, almost like she was skipping.

"What are you doing?" Anya asked.

"It's my happy skip," Drea said.

"Creepy," Anya said.

"I wouldn't do it on tile floors. You're probably damaging all your joints," I said.

Drea didn't stop. She was very hoppy all the way to the gym. Once we got to the gym, most of the eighth graders were already seated in the bleachers and the rest of the sixth and seventh graders were filing in. It was hard to feel excited about what was happening because I was so nervous. I hoped that the kids at my school would appreciate our presentation. A part of me feared they might hate it. Or think it was stupid. Or loudly boo at us. Any of those responses would've really devastated me.

Principal Hunt stood in front of the microphone and welcomed everybody.

"Yearbooks last forever. They are one of the few things you will keep until the day you die," she said.

I was really surprised she said it that way. It was rare that people brought up the day you'd die in middle school.

"So take what our staff is saying very seriously. They're experts. They're here to help you," Ms. Hunt said. "Please welcome your yearbook's senior photography editor, Javier Zuniga."

Javier looked spooked. He stood behind the microphone stand and fumbled through the papers.

"Um, I'm Javier," he said. "Um, my last name is, um, my last name is . . ."

"Zuniga!" a voice shouted from the crowd.

"He's choking," Anya said. "Should I go up there?"

I was afraid to tell her yes. I really wanted Javier to pull it together. He was our leader. I didn't want him to fail. Then, the unthinkable happened. Drea approached the microphone. I knew people recognized her, because I heard some fake puking sounds coming from somewhere in the back row.

"I'm Drea," she said. "Some of you know me from Marching Band. Some of you know me from the Internet."

I stared at Venice, thinking, Should we do something? Neither one of us did.

"I'm really excited about this clinic today. Know why? Because I have a terrible smile. I look forty percent uglier when I do this." Drea smiled her awkward smile for the school. It was sort of admirable, how she didn't seem to mind what people thought of her. I mean, as soon as I heard the boys fake-puking in the back, I probably would've taken my seat and felt terrible about myself for the rest of the day. But not Drea.

"So I'm here to get some tips on how to make my sixth-grade portrait look awesome. And Rocky Mountain Middle School's photography team is going to help us do that. Let's give it up for Venice Garcia, Perry Hall, Anya O'Shea, and Javier Zuniga."

The gymnasium let loose a smattering of applause. Which impressed me. It was crazy that Drea was able to do that introduction without notes. Javier had great notes and he hadn't been able to do anything besides mumble and sway from side to side. I guess being in the band all those years had taught Drea to be comfortable in front of a crowd.

Venice followed her up to the microphone. She cleared her throat. "We all want to take good pictures. But let's go ahead and look at some terrible ones first."

Venice had found these photos on the Internet. We felt it would be way too cruel to use our actual classmates for the "This Is Terrible" section of our presentation. In the first photo a woman aggressively showed all her teeth. It was a huge relief when I heard laughter coming from the crowd. Venice clicked to the next photo. A man's eyebrows were crooked and filled with wild, curly hairs. More laughter.

In the third photo a girl's eyes were almost crossed and looking the wrong direction. I heard a gasp. I supposed we'd accidentally freaked somebody out. In the fourth photo a man had lowered his head to look at the camera and had created a very unattractive triple chin. The crowd loved that one. Tons of people laughed. In the last photo a woman's whole face looked painted on with makeup. It got huge laughs. When it came to cracking up at unfortunate-looking people's photos, my middle school had really nailed it.

Venice waited for everybody to stop laughing before she spoke again. "What Perry tells you next will save you from taking a bad picture. So please listen."

The gymnasium fell silent. I was so nervous standing in front of the microphone that my knees felt wobbly. "Hello, everybody," I said. My voice echoed like I was inside a cave. I could feel how bored everybody felt. It was awful. "I am going to tell you five things that will help you look good. Drea, please help me demonstrate."

Drea hopped right over to me. I heard a few people laugh. I guessed watching Drea bounce around in boots was funnier than I had realized.

"Drea is wearing clothes that will photograph nicely. She's not wearing crazy patterns. And she's taken into consideration that our backdrop will be cream-colored. So she's wearing green. If she wears something too light you won't be able to separate her from the background, giving the illusion of a floating head."

Javier clicked on the next photo. It was a picture of Drea in a cream-colored sweater; her head appeared to float against the background.

"Cool!" a random boy yelled.

"And you want to make sure that you sit on the edge of your chair and look up toward the camera. Slumping looks bad," I said.

A picture of Drea slumping with a double chin flashed behind us. Javier got ahead of me and clicked on to the third photo before I was ready. It was a picture of Drea staring really intently at the camera, like a stalker.

"Scary!" a voice yelled.

Drea made the exact face again, making lots of people in the audience laugh.

"My advice to avoid this look is, keep your eyes closed right until I take the picture. That way you open your eyes and your whole face looks natural," I explained.

I caught a glimpse of Anya. She was rolling her eyes at everything I said, like all my advice was a complete waste of time. She really was not a team player. Javier clicked to the next picture before I was ready again. It showed Drea's hair with a bunch of flyaways.

"Bring a comb and be yourself," I said. "You don't want to make any drastic changes before your portrait. But you want to look your best. We'll help with that. But also try to angle your head up. You'll look better. I promise," I said.

The last picture was actually a series of pictures, one after the other, of Drea smiling.

"My last piece of advice is, practice," I said. "You'll feel more comfortable in front of the camera. And you'll also learn what looks best."

I was trying to think of one final thing to say when Anya rushed up to the microphone.

"I have a couple of things I'd like to add," Anya blurted out. "Wear good lip gloss. Seriously. Your mouth matters."

I saw Javier flipping through the outline, trying to find where it said Anya was supposed to be up there.

"Do it with your friends," Anya said. "They'll be the most honest about when you look bad. Or if your hair's doing something weird. Or if you've got a booger."

The audience laughed.

"Yeah," Anya said. "Nobody wants to see your nose funk."

I felt myself backing up until I was standing right next to Venice.

"Wow," I whispered to her.

"Stop her," Venice whispered back.

But I really didn't know how to do that in front of the whole school. Also, wasn't that Javier's job? Was our leader going to do *anything* during the assembly?

"Whatever you do," Anya said, "don't wear puffy sleeves. Also, chew gum. It will relax your face."

This is when I realized that Anya was dressed like a total villain. She was wearing black jeans, a slim black belt, and a tucked-in black shirt with crocheted sleeves. It didn't matter that her boots were purple; she looked very sinister. I watched Principal Hunt approach the microphone. Was she aware that Anya had gone rogue? Had her evil outfit given her away? Was Principal Hunt going to stop her? She leaned down to speak into the microphone.

"Gum isn't allowed in school. But I do think you should wear comfortable shoes," Principal Hunt said. "You should not only look your best, you should also feel your best. I find that really helps me take a good picture."

"Totally," Anya said, leaning into the microphone again. "And don't wear a ton of jewelry. It pulls attention away from your face."

"And make sure you get a good night's sleep the night before," Principal Hunt said. "You don't want circles under your eyes."

Javier looked like he was losing his mind. We'd gone very far away from the outline.

"We've exceeded our ten tips. This is too much advice," Venice said. "Nobody will be able to remember it all."

"This is a terrible clinic," I mumbled to Venice.

She gave me her worried face and then gritted her teeth. Which didn't solve anything.

"Don't wear white," Anya said. "It will make your skin look gray. And also, start with a cleansed face and try to use a matte foundation. No shimmery bronzers."

"They look so bored," Venice said. "And she's only speaking to the girls now. What about the boys?"

I scanned the audience. Seeing my whole school bored and uncomfortable, sandwiched into the wooden bleachers, made me feel really deflated about my current life goal to make them all look good in their portraits. Even though our clinic had turned weird and endless, I felt they still should have been paying more attention. But everybody was whispering to one another. And I doubted it was about Anya's styling tips.

"And if you contour, which I don't recommend, make sure it's fully blended. I think it goes without saying that you need to make sure your neck and your face are the same color," Anya went on.

"I should tackle her," I said to Venice. "I should grab her

by one of her crocheted sleeves and throw her down to the floor."

"You don't want to get detention again," Venice said, putting her arm in front of me to hold me back.

"Fill in your eyebrows if they're light—they'll show up better on camera," Anya said. "And don't wear anything that will go out of style in a year. This tip also applies to accessories. A pair of stud earrings is enough."

I noticed Mr. Falconer standing in the corner next to the American flag. He was swiping away on his phone. I'd never seen him on his phone before. I took it as a sign that our clinic had turned dull and unwatchable.

"I'll just go tap her on the shoulder," I said.

"That won't do anything," Venice said. "She'll ignore you."

"Don't match your hair to your shirt," Anya said. "And avoid full-frontal pictures. Only give a three-quarter face angle. But you should practice this with a digital camera at home."

"Okay. I'm just going to grab the microphone," I said. "If I take it and run out of the gymnasium, won't that mean the assembly is over?"

Venice squeezed her lips together and looked very unsure, like she was doing an extremely hard math problem in her head.

"Don't let yourself get distracted by anything," Anya said. "If there's a bee, it's dead to you. Somebody farts? Ignore it."

A few boys laughed, which surprised me. I'd figured everybody had stopped paying attention when she mentioned filling in your eyebrows. Okay. Okay. Okay. It was now or never. I started walking toward Anya and the microphone.

"Try to smile with your eyes," Anya said. "And look above the camera lens instead of right at it, and extend your neck."

I stood right next to Anya and whispered in her ear, "You need to stop right now."

"And for those of you with acne, blend your pimple cream," Anya said. "You want to look timeless and classy."

"I mean it," I whispered.

"And here's Perry Hall," Anya said.

I felt everybody's attention fall on me. I held my breath. Anya had said my name as if she was going to say something about me. What was she going to say?

"See how her barrettes pull her hair back unevenly, giving her head an asymmetrical shape?" As Anya spoke I felt her fingertip graze my ear. "You definitely want to avoid that mistake. You want your head to look round and normal."

I heard some kids chuckle. My face and neck felt very hot.

"Thank you, Rocky Mountain Middle School. Now let's all show up looking gorgeous for our portraits." Anya gave her hand a kiss and pretended to throw it toward the audience. Then she smiled big and sat down, leaving me in front of the empty microphone, deeply worried about exactly how asymmetrical my head actually looked. With everybody staring at me, I wasn't sure what to say. I needed to figure out a good way to end things. All of a sudden, I felt somebody standing next to me. It was Javier. Finally, our leader had arrived.

"Thanks, everybody, for coming," Javier said.

I stood there stunned, waiting for Javier to say something way better. But that didn't happen. The room filled with the sound of people fleeing the gym. The assembly was over.

Everybody was going back to class. I watched them trudge across the floor. What a wasted opportunity.

There was no way everybody would be able to remember all those tips. Anya had ruined the assembly. She'd purposely overwhelmed the crowd and then insulted me. Worst of all, other than the mean thing she said about my barrettes, I didn't think her tips were sincere. I didn't think she really wanted the geeks to look better or for the nerds to blend their pimple cream. She was just showing off. She'd grabbed the spotlight and torpedoed my photo clinic. And she'd done it in a very sneaky and mean way. She'd waited for Javier to flounder and then she'd pounced, finding the perfect moment to humiliate me in front of everybody.

Anya was such a snake. I had no idea how to even exist with her anymore.

12

The Purge

Things turned bad for me all the time. It was the way my life worked. It wasn't fair, but I was getting used to it. Good things turned bad. Medium-okay things turned bad. And bad things turned rotten. So it was inevitable that things at home would turn bad. And when they did it was swift and permanent.

"This is going to change our lives," my mother said, opening up the pantry.

Normally, I enjoyed Friday nights. Normally, I loved it when Piper came home to visit. But ever since the garage fight nothing had been normal with Piper. My mom had been texting my sister every day, asking her to come home so they could work things out. So I guessed this was Piper's version of working things out.

Piper stood beside my mother with a giant garbage bag. My dad and I sat at the kitchen table, where we could examine everything in our cupboards.

"I don't want to sound like I'm judging you guys," Piper

said. "But you're filthy eaters. Look at all this processed food. It's crap."

I watched Piper shove a bag of marshmallows into the trash bag. It made me sad to see them go.

"I'm all for cleaner eating," my dad said. "But shouldn't we spend a week eating what we've got instead of chucking it into the landfill?"

Piper frowned at him, and so did my mother.

"That's your sugar addiction talking, Dad," Piper said. "Stay strong."

She forcefully threw out a whole box of graham crackers.

"I agree with Piper," my mom said. "Lately, I just haven't been feeling like myself. We should be eating more fruits and vegetables. Piper sent me an article explaining how this stuff alters our mood, even our behavior."

I glanced at my dad. I thought he'd take a stand in the name of dentistry against that article and make some argument about how some of these foods were actually good for our teeth. For instance, all the sugar-free instant pudding Piper had just thrown away. Wasn't soft, sugarless food something we should keep around?

It was like a tragic parade. Everything I loved got tossed into the trash right in front of me. My favorite pretzels. My favorite chocolate chips. Even my favorite gummy fruit snacks.

"Why can't you just eat a strawberry?" Piper asked, wagging the gummy snacks in my face before she dropped them into the bag.

I shrugged. "Those have vitamin D in them and are chewier."

Piper and I both knew the reason I ate gummies had

nothing to do with vitamin D. When Piper opened up our fridge my dad got a little anxious. He leaned forward and spoke pretty firmly.

"We are keeping all the cheese," he said. "I'm not going to get into a fight about it."

"Your body would feel so much better if you gave it a dairy break," Piper encouraged.

"She's right," my mom said. "Two days ago I switched cow milk for almond milk and my energy levels have soared." She shot her hand into the air like it was a plane. My dad was not convinced.

"The cheese stays," he said.

Piper pulled out a hunk of white cheese wrapped in a plastic baggie. "This has mold on it." She pinched her nose with two fingers and dangled the cheese over the trash bag.

"I don't care," my dad said. "I'll cut around it."

My eyes grew wide when he said that. I wanted to take his side, because I knew he really liked cheese. But once it grew mold I thought it was time to get that cheese out of the refrigerator.

"Piper," my dad said sternly. "You're hardly ever at home. You spend ninety percent of your time studying and eating salads with Bobby. This is our food. I just don't understand why *we* need to change."

My dad was still in the dark about so much. Because of his heavy work schedule he remained unaware of all the Bobby/Thailand tension in our house. He didn't understand that the real reason my mom was letting Piper throw away all our artificially flavored food was that she was trying to lure Piper into spending more time with us and less time with Bobby-the-bad-influence boyfriend. My mom thought if she could keep Piper happy, she could keep Piper here. But I wasn't sure that was going to happen. The more I looked at Piper, the easier it was for me to picture her in Thailand. Maybe that had something to do with the fact that she was wearing a pashmina shawl.

"I'm doing this because I love you guys and I'm worried about how this crap is going to affect you down the line. Studies show this garbage turns your brain to mush." Piper threw out an unopened jar of bright-orange cheese.

"That's being a little hyperbolic," my dad said.

But I actually found that jar of cheese very frightening. It was *so* orange.

"What will we eat for snacks?" my dad asked when Piper tossed out several bags of unpopped microwave popcorn.

"Edamame!" my mother cheered, opening the freezer and lifting up a small bag emblazoned with a healthy red heart and what I assumed were dancing green beans.

My father looked at me mournfully. "We'll give it a week and see how we feel, okay?"

I shrugged. If I was really craving some crap food, I could ask Venice to bring me some. And Hayes, even though I didn't want him to, would give me a coconut ball every now and then. This good-food purge seemed survivable. Especially if it made Piper happy.

"Dad," Piper said solemnly. "Do I need to go through your car?"

My dad looked panicked and waved her off. "The car is fine. There's nothing much in there."

My mom and Piper looked at each other very doubtfully.

"Isn't that where you keep your salty licorice stash?" Piper asked him.

Poor guy. It was going to be hard for him to lose that stash. He loved salty licorice.

"Many cultures feel licorice has medicinal properties," my dad said. "The stash stays."

"I was afraid you'd say that," Piper said, lifting a twist-tied baggie up from behind the counter. "That's why I went and got it as soon as you parked the car."

My dad stood up. "That stuff is from Sweden. It's not cheap!"

Piper tossed it into the trash. It was sort of amazing to observe. I'd never seen her act this hostile before.

"You should let him keep it," my mom said. "We all need a guilty pleasure. I'm keeping my breath mints."

Piper tried to run and drag the bag with her, but it was too big. My dad caught her and reached inside the trash and pulled out his salty licorice. It was a stunning and disgusting thing to witness.

"It's done," my father said sternly. "The purge is over. We'll eat a little healthier, but we're not going to change overnight."

Piper looked like she was on the verge of tears. "It's like you shipped me off to college to grow and become a brand-new person and you guys want to stay exactly who you are. It's not fair!"

"Don't look at it that way," my mom said. "We're just old and we like who we are. But we're trying our best."

Piper looked at me like she wanted me to offer her support. I shrugged and said, "I'm twelve. I'm supposed to like sugar."

Normally, Piper would have stormed off and gone back to college. But the night of the purge was different. On the night of the purge something else happened.

Ding-dong. Ding-dong.

"I'll get it," Piper said. "I'd hate for anybody to have to *change* where they're standing."

I tried not to feel bad about Piper's comments. Because I thought they were mostly aimed at my parents. I was just an innocent bystander.

"Yes," Piper said. "I've got a box for you."

I couldn't hear what the person at the door was saying. I thought it was weird that Piper would be giving them a box.

"Now is not a good time," Piper said. "Wait here and I'll get Perry."

What? My sister gave somebody a box? And that person wanted to see me? Could it be Bobby? Why would Bobby want to see me? Who was at the door?

"Perry," Piper said, whooshing back into the kitchen, "Drea wants to see you."

It was like a nightmare had knocked on my very own front door. I was so sick of Drea Quan. The last place I wanted her to be was on my doorstep.

"You really need to let us know if you're inviting friends over," my dad said.

I opened my mouth and looked at him in horror. "She's not my friend. She's the hot dog puker."

"That's so mean," Piper said. "Give the girl a break."

"Perry," my mom said harshly. "Go to the door, she's waiting."

I reluctantly scooted my chair back and stood up. And I hesitantly walked to my front door. It was unbelievable. Under my porch light, holding a big box, stood a smiling Drea Quan.

"Hey," Drea said. Her smile was enormous and her lips had on a normal amount of berry gloss. "I didn't want to leave without saying hey."

"Hey," I said in a slightly hostile voice.

"Let me know if you need anything," Drea said. "I know I've gotten a few follow-up questions after the assembly."

"You did?" I asked. Because that was my photo clinic. If people had questions they should have been sending them to me.

"Yeah, I think Anya spurted out way too much information," Drea said. "Some of the kids in Band were confused about whether puffy sleeves were good or bad. And they didn't understand why they should look above the camera. Don't worry, I explained everything."

I was so angry. I was angry that Drea was here. I was angry that she was stealing my follow-up questions. And I was angry that my marshmallows were in the bottom of a trash bag.

"You should forward those questions to me," I said. "I'm in charge of the portraits." My voice was very stern and I didn't look happy.

Drea shifted the box onto her hip. It must've been heavier than I realized. "Oh. Wow. Sorry," she said. "I'll do that from now on. I was just trying to help."

But her comment did not take away my anger. "You're actually making more work for me." Because what if she wasn't telling these kids the exact right thing? They'd show up doing everything wrong. I couldn't deal with that. I didn't deserve to have to put in any additional work.

"Anything else?" I asked. I was being so rude and I didn't even care.

"Um," Drea said, looking very uncomfortable, "can you thank Piper again for the clothes?"

No way. Was that what was in the box? Piper's clothes? It blew my mind. I really didn't understand why Piper would be doing this. Even if she wanted to go to Thailand, didn't I deserve her clothes? Hadn't I earned them by being her sister for twelve years? Wasn't that worth anything to her?

"I'll tell her," I said. And then before Drea could say one more word I shut the door. And I didn't do it softly. I banged that sucker shut as hard as I could. And then through the door, I heard Drea's awful voice. What was she saying? I couldn't quite hear. I really wanted to keep the door closed even if it meant I was the rudest person in the world. But some part of my brain insisted on being kind and opened it anyway. Also, I thought I heard her mention our principal.

"What?" I asked.

"That stuff Anya said about your head. About it looking wonky and asymmetrical. A couple of kids in Band felt that was super snarky and wanted to write and complain to Principal Hunt about it. Are you cool with that?"

I couldn't believe Drea Quan was standing on my doorstep bringing up my head shape! I'd barely just stopped obsessing over it, after Venice sent me twenty pictures of myself to show that my head looked round no matter how I wore my barrettes.

"Complaining about Anya doesn't solve anything," I said. "I think it only makes her stronger."

"So you don't care—" Drea started to ask me something, but I cut her off. I'd heard enough.

"I don't care at all," I said, reslamming the door, and this time hurrying away from it before Drea could say something else that would trick me into opening it.

When I stormed back to the kitchen, Piper was helping my mom cut bell peppers. I was seething. I felt hurt and betrayed and confused.

"Why are you giving Drea your clothes?" I asked.

Piper tossed some pepper cubes into a big bowl of lettuce. "She asked for them."

"Wait," I said. "Some random sixth grader asks you for your clothes and you just box them up and hand them over?"

Piper set down the knife and looked at me with a disappointed face. "That girl is fifty times the nerd you are. Show some empathy," Piper said. "She'll make full use of those eight shirts, three skirts, and two pairs of leggings."

I felt dizzy. My sister had betrayed me more than I realized. That was basically an entire wardrobe.

"I would never go behind your back like that," I said. "I would check with you first before I interfered with people at your school!"

And then I turned to go down my hallway.

"That girl has sent me so many nice pops about you. She totally looks up to you," Piper said. "It's nuts that you're mad at her."

I flipped around. "I don't care what she pops about me. I can't stand that girl!"

"Wait," my dad said. "Don't yell at your sister."

It was quite a surprise that my dad was siding with Piper. Especially since he didn't even know half of what was happening.

"It's okay, Dad," Piper said, walking toward me. "I think I know what Perry's real issue is here."

How dare Piper speak for me or my real issue! I was speechless.

"When did our lives descend into so much drama?" my mother asked. "Fifth grade didn't feel like this."

My mom was really speaking the truth with that comment. Back in fifth grade, Piper still lived with us and was an awesome sister. I didn't have to share Venice with Leo. I didn't have thirty-eight tasks. And I didn't have to deal with Drea Quan and Anya O'Shea either. Now, it felt like that was all I did at school.

"Perry is jealous," Piper said.

And that made my jaw drop. Why was Piper being so critical of me?

"I am not jealous of Drea Quan!" I said, folding my arms across my chest and releasing a sound of disgust.

"But you are," Piper said, pointing her finger at me in a stabby way. "You're jealous that Drea and Venice and I and everybody else you know is on PopRat. It eats you up and you feel left behind that you're not sending pops."

First, at my own clinic, I was used as an example of having a wonky head. Then a nerd came to my house to remind me of this sad fact. Finally, my sister stood in our living room calling me a lame, jealous person because I wasn't on PopRat. I couldn't take it anymore. It was too much. I burst into tears.

"Perry wants a rat?" my dad asked.

My mother groaned and wrapped her arms around me, giving me a big hug.

"These apps come and go, leaving a path of destruction in the lives of everybody who uses them," she said, trying to rock me into a calmer state.

"PopRat is actually a ton of fun," Piper said. "Even Bobby's on it."

My mother scowled at Piper. "Your sister isn't getting it."

"Now I know what you're talking about," my dad said. "All the dental hygienists in the office use it. There's a filter that turns you into a guinea pig, right?"

I sniffled and relaxed into my mom's hug. That sounded like an amazing filter. I bet Venice and Leo were using that all the time.

"Don't turn me into the bad guy," my mom said. "We both agreed when we got Perry her phone: no messaging apps."

"Did we?" my dad asked.

And even though I was still terribly upset, I saw a sliver of hope in what was happening.

"If you shelter Perry too much, you'll turn her into a freak," Piper said. "Just make her add you to her sewer. You can keep tabs on her."

"Nobody is getting added into anybody's sewer," my mom said. "Perry is lucky she even has a phone."

And that comment frightened me a little bit, because I couldn't even picture my life without my phone. The next ten minutes were a very heated argument between my mom and

Piper. Basically, my dad and I sat on the sidelines. I thought it was pretty clear we were both pro-PopRat.

Piper: Teach her how to use it responsibly.
Mom: Impossible. You send the wrong thing one time and your life gets ruined.
Piper: Give Perry more credit than that.
Mom: You're not her mother. I am!
Piper: I love Perry just as much as you do. And you're preventing her from experiencing something culturally important. You can't build a tech fence around her and keep her safe forever.

And when my mom didn't spit back an automatic reply to Piper's "tech fence" comment, I saw my chance.

"I would be so responsible," I said. "I'd really only pop with Venice."

"I can't believe Mrs. Garcia lets Venice pop at all," my mother said.

"It does seem fun," my dad said. "It's basically the same thing as sending texts and photos, which we already let Perry do."

"Again," I said, "I'd be *soooo* responsible."

I thought I saw the exact moment in my mother's face when she cracked. Piper had broken her argument down. I glanced at Piper and she winked at me. It was really hard to hate her, even though she was helping Drea.

"What happens if she adds me to her sewer?" my mom asked.

"It means you get to see everything that goes in her trash.

And pops move into your trash right after you read them, unless you relocate them to your nest. But you can make her add you there, too. I mean, you'll need a different user name. No one person can be in your sewer and your nest. It's not how it works. But maybe Dad could be in her nest and you could be in her sewer. You'd get to see everything."

"That's more phone supervision than she gets now," my dad said.

Piper sneaked up behind me and gave me a hug. But I was actually a little nervous about adding my parents to my sewer and my nest. Because I didn't want them looking at all my texts and photos that I sent to Venice.

Piper could tell I was nervous about this. "Don't worry," she said. "Either Venice or I will show you the ropes."

"I'll need somebody to show me the ropes too," my mom said.

"Add me to the tutorial," my dad said.

"But I don't want Mom and Dad reading every pop I send," I whispered to Piper.

Piper smiled and then whispered, "They won't see anything you send. It's only the incoming stuff that gets sent to your sewer and nest."

"Oh," I said. "Awesome."

"Remember this, Perry Hall. Your sister loves you. She looks out for you. And even when you think I'm not paying attention to your problems, I'm probably in the other room, trying to solve everything from there."

I felt like crying again. And not like before, when I wanted to hurry to my bed and crawl under the cover because I hated sixth grade and felt the nerds were too difficult to rescue. I wanted to cry because Piper had done something that was going to change my life. I was getting PopRat. Venice wouldn't be popping without me anymore. Nobody would. Finally, I'd be part of the party. Finally, it would be easier to be me.

13

Brain Freeze

When my mom dropped me off at Fro-yo Unicorn to take pictures for the What's Hot section, she gave me strict instructions. "Text me as soon as you're done. And don't eat too much sugar."

"Frozen yogurt is healthy," I reassured her. It was one of the few things in the freezer that my sister had let us keep. "Piper says it has probiotics in it."

"I'm worried about the toppings," my mom said, squeezing her eyebrows together in concern.

"You worry too much," I said.

But I guessed she didn't want to hear that, because she squeezed her eyebrows together extra hard and said, "My biggest worry right now is that Yearbook has turned into a giant time suck for our entire family. And now we've got to learn how to PopRat."

"Whoa," I said. Because it really surprised me that my mom had used the word *suck*. Also, I was pretty sure PopRat would make all our lives better.

"I'll probably only be an hour," I said. But really, she made a good point. Doing classwork for Yearbook on a Saturday was a drag.

"Okay. I'll just swing by in an hour," my mom said.

"Don't do that," I said. "I might have to take pictures of fennel sausage next door."

My mother rummaged through her purse. "Why does a middle-school yearbook need pictures of meat products?" she asked. "It just feels wrong."

"It really does," I agreed.

Then she handed me five bucks. "Text me the moment you finish."

"Got it," I said. I wasn't sure when my mom and I would completely regain each other's trust. But at moments like this it was obvious she hadn't forgotten that I'd recently been given detention *and* superglued a map of Idaho to my face.

I hopped out of the car and hurried into the shop. Taking pictures always improved my mood.

"Over here, Perry!" Javier called as I walked through the door.

He was standing next to Fro-yo Unicorn's manager, Janet. I knew this because she was wearing a name tag that read I'M JANET, FRO-YO UNICORN MANAGER. There were a bunch of cups of frozen yogurt piled in front of them. Jessi was already here too. She was sitting in a booth cradling her neon-pink cast.

"Am I late?" I asked. Because I thought I was exactly on time.

"Javier asked me to get here early," Jessi said. She grabbed a gummy bear from a small paper cup. It looked delicious.

"Don't eat the props!" Javier said.

"It's okay," the manager said. "I can get you more of those."

Jessi popped several more into her mouth.

"Aren't we shooting Fletcher and Reece too?" I asked.

I thought we were shooting all the What's Hot section at the same time. And since they'd won for seventh and eighth grades, I'd figured they'd be here.

"Fletcher's hair was way too spiky," Javier explained. "So I sent him to the bathroom to fix it. And I asked Reece to put on some lip gloss. Venice is helping her. She looked so pale."

"Venice is already here?" I asked. I was surprised she hadn't texted me the second she walked through the door.

"Over here!" Venice called.

I turned and saw her in the corner, gently applying a lipstick wand to Reece's smile. I'd shown up on time, but everything had already started. I guessed Javier was feeling the need to impress everybody after he bombed at the assembly. I got it. But I wished he'd told me to get here early too.

I was trotting over to join Venice when I heard Javier call to me, "No, Perry. We need you over here. Can you help Anya set up the props?"

I stopped. Anya? Last I'd heard, she was too busy to come. Why hadn't anybody warned me she'd be here? I glared at Javier. And then I glared at Venice. Because it really bothered me to have my enemy sprung on me like this at a yogurt shop after what had happened at the assembly.

"I've got it," Anya said. "What do you think?"

I turned the corner and saw Anya O'Shea standing beside a back booth. I watched her scatter rainbow sprinkles over a mound of pink frozen yogurt.

"I thought fudgy banana marshmallow fluff was the favorite topping," I said. Why was she putting sprinkles on the yogurt?

Javier came rushing up. "Why are there sprinkles over everything?"

"They're pretty," Anya said, smiling and dropping more onto the yogurt.

"Stop!" Javier looked panicked. "We need another cup!"

"I guess I'll have to eat this one," Anya said, taking a giant bite.

"Perry, can you handle this?" Javier asked.

"Sure," I said.

I watched Javier run off into the bathroom.

"He's a legit mess," Anya said.

I felt somebody touch me and I jumped. Luckily it was Venice.

"It's been total chaos since I got here," she said.

But that seemed weird to me. Because how hard was it to take a few pictures in a frozen yogurt shop? Why couldn't Javier pull this shoot together?

"When are you going to take my picture?" Jessi hollered. "I'm getting brain freeze."

"Wow," I said. "Jessi is turning purple."

"Oh no. It's the huckleberry sauce," Venice said. "It's stained her mouth. Javier told her not to eat it."

Why was that even on the table? All we needed was the fudgy banana marshmallow fluff. It was as if I were the only person who understood that fudgy banana marshmallow fluff had won What's Hot. And the only reason any of us were here was to photograph it.

"Stop eating the sauce!" Javier said. "You look like a zombie."

That was not a nice thing to tell a person before you took her picture. You were supposed to flatter her and make her feel relaxed.

"Where's the equipment?" I asked Javier. Even though he already seemed stressed out, I needed to know. Because I had to put on the portrait lens.

"Ask Anya," Javier said, scrambling over a booth to talk to Reece.

"I didn't realize he was so scattered," Venice said.

First the assembly and now this. Either Javier really crumbled under pressure, or Anya was secretly making him crash and burn. I suspected the latter.

Fletcher came out of the bathroom, and his hair definitely didn't look too spiky. It looked totally flat.

Javier noticed and smacked his forehead.

"Why do you look so weird?" Javier asked Fletcher.

Again, not a nice thing to tell a person right before you photographed him. Anya was laughing. She was a master of creating chaos. I wondered what her parents were like. Seriously. Where had Anya learned her weasel tactics?

"I still don't know where the camera is," I said. "Nothing can happen until I put on the portrait lens."

"Anya!" Javier yelled.

It was like she'd disappeared. Which I wouldn't have minded. Except I needed the equipment.

"We need pink lip gloss for Jessi," Venice said. "We have to cover up the purple."

"You fix that," Javier said. "I'll fix Fletcher. Perry, go find Anya."

It was like I'd been given the worst job ever.

"My mom is going to be here soon," Jessi said. "I didn't know it would take this long."

It really upset me that she was complaining. Derby wouldn't have complained. He would have been super easy to work with and done everything we asked. And if Javier had said "Don't eat the purple sauce," Derby would not have eaten the purple sauce. Hot people, it turned out, were very difficult to work with.

"Anya?" I called as I wandered through the yogurt shop. "Anya?" She wasn't anywhere. Not in the bathroom. Or under any of the tables. But the camera bag was.

"I found the equipment, but I didn't find Anya," I said.

Javier looked so relieved. Luckily, he'd fixed Fletcher's hair, glossed Reece's pale face, and de-purpled Jessi's mouth. Maybe he was a better leader under pressure than I'd given him credit for.

"Great," Javier said. "One more thing. And I don't want you to take this the wrong way."

"Okay," I said.

"Don't take crappy pictures."

Wow. That really stung. I always took awesome pictures. I thought Javier could tell he'd hurt my feelings by the way I curled my lips in total horror and confusion.

"What I mean is that I want you to try to take the best pictures possible. Don't take bad pictures because you're upset that your friends lost and didn't make it into the section." He gave me a big frown. "Don't go into this with a secret agenda to torpedo What's Hot."

Javier really blew my mind with that comment. First, I would never take a bad picture on purpose. I was an artist. I aimed to take perfect shots every time. Second, I didn't think any of my "friends" had lost. Derby was a geek and I had rooted for him, but he wasn't my friend. Third, I didn't have an agenda. And I especially didn't have a secret one that I planned to use as a torpedo. Fourth, wasn't Javier smart enough to realize that Anya was behind this meltdown?

"Um," I said, "I take awesome photos. That's why Ms. Kenny made me junior photographer."

And that was when I saw a wave of relief wash over Javier's face and he broke out in a relaxed smile. "I knew Anya was just messing with me."

Anya O'Shea really needed to get a life. And stay far, far away from mine.

"Brain freeze!" Jessi yelled, pushing away a pink cup.

"Jessi!" Javier scolded. "You need to look normal. Stop eating the yogurt."

But I thought it would be pretty funny if Jessi had brain-freeze face for her photo.

It was almost like Javier could read my mind.

"Do not take her picture until her face returns to its normal color," Javier snapped.

He was really uptight. Venice looked at me with a ton of sympathy. And I appreciated that.

When things were over I was super hopeful that Venice and I could hang out and eat some marshmallow fluff and talk about our lives. She would flip when I told her about Piper, and the food purge, and Drea coming over and getting clothes. But just then Venice's phone buzzed.

"It's Leo," she said.

And I tried to keep myself from making a gagging sound.

"Don't do that," Venice said.

We were such good friends that I didn't even need to make the gagging sound. She could tell that was how I truly felt.

"When you get a boyfriend I'm not going to hate on him," Venice said.

It made me feel really weird when she said that. Why would I want a boyfriend? My life was great. I didn't need that. I didn't even like anybody. Did she think that I liked somebody?

"Stop making that face," Venice said.

And so I tried to make my face look like my normal face.

"Leo's mom brought Leo over to say hello," Venice said. "I'll be right back."

And Venice bounced right out of the store. And that just left me and Javier and a million things to do. Luckily, I was great at my job.

Once she stopped being purple, I took an amazing photo of Jessi. And I snapped an awesome picture of Reece. And Fletcher looked very hot and gorgeous, just like out of a magazine, and I didn't have to give him any guidance at all. His picture looked awesome and he knew it. What a professional.

It wasn't until it was time to take a picture of the fudgy banana marshmallow fluff that things turned bad.

"Hi, Perry," a bouncy voice called.

I turned around. It was Drea. And she was wearing one of Piper's shirts. And a pair of Piper's leggings. I almost fell over.

It was like she'd shown up and rubbed my sister's clothes right in my face.

"Perry!" another chipper voice called.

I turned and looked in the other direction. It was Hayes. He was standing in the yogurt shop. And he was trying to hand me something. I couldn't believe it. More skating passes! What was wrong with him?

"Cool, are those skating passes?" Javier asked.

But I just stood there and looked at everybody like I was shocked to death. Because I was.

Javier said, "I know you're trying to get a good picture of Drea for Yearbook, so I thought you could take one of her eating the fudgy banana marshmallow fluff. No reason to take a picture of the topping by itself. And I asked Hayes to come for the fennel sausage topping. You can thank me later." Then he winked at me. Then Hayes winked at me. And I turned to look at Drea and she had a terrible smile on her face. And then Anya popped around the corner eating a giant pink cone of frozen yogurt. It was like I was trapped inside a nightmare, except I was wide-awake.

"Let's get this over with," I said. I glanced out the window to see if Venice was coming, but she was laughing on the sidewalk with Leo. It looked like they were eating a giant pretzel. Ugh! Where was my best friend when I needed her? Not standing next to me in Fro-yo Unicorn, that much was certain.

When Venice *and* Leo finally tumbled back into the store, it was like they were a human ball of laughter. I didn't even know for sure if Venice was breathing, she was laughing that hard.

"Are you guys finished?" Leo asked. "Do you need any help?"

I was already putting the camera back in its case. It was pretty obvious I didn't need help.

"Perry knocked this shoot out of the park," Javier said. "You are a Party."

And it sort of surprised me to hear my secret nickname used in public.

"We only call her that in Yearbook," Anya said.

"Your nickname is Party?" Drea asked. "That's so cool!"

I rolled my eyes. I didn't need Drea to give me any compliments.

"You should bring your party to the skating rink," Hayes said.

And that totally freaked me out to be put on the spot like that.

"I would love to go skating," Venice said.

"We should do it," Leo said. "How many passes do you have?"

I pulled the tickets out of my pocket and counted them. "Four."

"Just tell me when you guys want to come," Hayes said. "I can get you all in."

"Even my brother?" Venice asked. "He's been dying to try your Rollerblade ramp."

"Yeah, I can do that," Hayes said. "Just have Perry call me or text me or whatever."

I glared at Venice. Why was she putting me in this situation? It was like she wanted me to go out with Hayes whether I liked him or not. Which felt very rude to me.

"Leo's mom is waiting," Venice said.

She gave me a quick hug and then grabbed Leo's hand and headed toward the door.

"Skating will be awesome!" Venice called.

A cluster of bells hanging on the door jingled as it closed.

"We're done," Javier said. "Mission accomplished."

Wow. That was how he felt? It was like Javier and I weren't even in the same place making the same yearbook. It was like we were living on two different planets.

14

Multiple Pens

I was so happy that Venice and I had settled on talking about Lake Pend Oreille, the largest lake in Idaho, for our oral report. Because our other choices—potatoes, trout, fur trade, tourism, geothermal water, precious and semiprecious stones, state seal designer Emma Edwards Green, and the invention of the Pulaski (a special hand tool used in wild-land firefighting)—hadn't really grabbed me.

Venice sat beside me on my bed as we leaned back on my pillows and zoomed through the Internet on my laptop, looking for reliable sources to quote. Mr. Falconer had a firm policy for all research projects, which required us to turn in a detailed list of all the sources we visited. And at least five had to be linked to official government pages, because he felt those gave out the best and most credible information.

But I wasn't so sure, because some guy named Hal who lived in Ketchum kept a blog about Idaho lakes. And he seemed to have way more usable information than the sites Mr. Falconer had recommended. Plus, Hal's came with awesome pictures of his dog, Skipper. As I read through Hal's blog, I wondered if Venice thought that too.

"So what do you think?" I asked, pointing to a photo of Skipper catching a Frisbee in front of a bunch of ponderosa pines.

"We can't use blogs," Venice said, sounding super judgy. "Leo said that last year when he did his report on fur trading, Mr. Falconer actually interrupted and told him that he was oversimplifying the early power struggles between the trappers. We don't want to use any questionably sourced info in case we get called out."

I blinked at Venice when she said this. Because it sort of broke my heart that on a night when we were hanging out in my bedroom for the first time in forever, working on a report about Lake Pend Oreille, she was thinking about Leo and his lame report on fur trading.

She didn't notice I was annoyed. "Leo actually made fur trading seem interesting. Did you know if it hadn't been for a sudden interest in wolverines and ringtail cats, the whole fur industry might have collapsed?"

It made me sad to think of all those furry animals being made into weird-looking hats and robes. But it made me even sadder that it felt like Leo was *almost* in my bedroom with us.

"Huh," I said, trying to effectively communicate how frustrated I was with her Leo tidbits.

"Seriously," Venice continued. "Leo explained to me how the discovery of the silkworm and Europeans' taste for softer top hats basically killed the entire beaver-trade industry in Idaho."

After she mentioned silkworms, I couldn't keep quiet about how I felt any longer.

"I think we should forget about beavers and forget about Leo," I said. Then I snapped my fingers to let her know I meant business.

"It's super rude to snap your fingers in somebody's face like that," Venice said, grimacing.

I put my hand down, because I wasn't trying to be *super* rude. I was actually trying to have a sincere conversation with her about how her boyfriend-mentioning behavior was wrecking both our sleepover and oral report progress.

"Venice," I said, clearing my throat and sitting up very straight so she'd understand I was being totally earnest. "We're finally hanging out and working on our report and Leo's not here. It's just the two of us. So maybe you could please start talking about Lake Pend Oreille. And all the secret submarine training they do there. Because listening to you talk about your boyfriend all the time is annoying."

After I finished talking I looked at Venice to see if I'd gotten through to her. Because it was really undeniable that Leo was taking up way too much of her headspace and free time. She took her hair out of her ponytail and shook it. Then she smoothed her thick brown hair into another tail, higher up on her head. She looked like she was still processing everything I'd said. I worried I'd upset her, but I also felt like I had a right to tell her how I really felt. She let out a big sigh.

"I thought you'd finished hating Leo," Venice finally said.

And that was a hard thing to hear. Because I had told her

that I'd stopped hating him. But weren't hate and annoyance two different things? And didn't she understand that when it was just the two of us hanging out, we should talk about non-Leo stuff? I wasn't sure how to tell her this any more clearly than I just had. But I took another crack at it.

"I feel like our friendship always came first." I held up my pointer finger to communicate the number one. "But now with Leo around I come second." I raised another finger.

Venice leaned forward and tried to protest but I stopped her.

"Leo totally comes first right now. You ride the bus together, hold hands, pop to each other nonstop, and you talk about him when he's not even here. And that's the part that hurts my feelings. Because I'm right here, Venice. It's me," I said, aiming my number one and number two fingers back at me. "Your best friend."

I was surprised when I heard my voice crack. But until this exact moment, with Venice sitting on my bed like old times, I hadn't realized how much I'd missed her.

"You need to stop," Venice said. "You're making me feel terrible!"

But that only made me feel sadder. Because didn't she realize that I felt terrible too? I felt my eyes getting hot. I couldn't stop myself. I started to sniffle. "So I'm not supposed to tell you how I feel?" I asked.

That was when I felt myself tumbling off the bed. Venice had scampered toward me to give me a hug, but I was too close to the edge and had toppled over. I opened my eyes. From my carpet I saw Venice's concerned face staring down at me.

"Perry, I need to tell you something," she said. Her ponytail slid over her shoulder and swung gently from side to side. "I feel so crappy."

I didn't say anything at first. Because she sure wasn't behaving like somebody who felt crappy. She was behaving like a person who had a terrific life and felt wonderful about it.

"I feel stuck," Venice said. "And I don't know what to do."

I couldn't believe I was finally hearing Venice say those words. Because it meant that Venice felt stuck in a relationship with Leo and that she wanted out! And while she might not have known what to do, I sure did. Venice needed to dump him. Right now. In my bedroom. She could use my phone. I couldn't stop myself from smiling.

"Don't look so happy," Venice said. "I've been feeling terrible ever since Leo started planning our Halloween costume. I should've talked about this with you sooner."

Wow. They were going to break up over his awful ideas for Halloween costumes. It was like a dream come true.

"It's okay," I said. "It's probably been an ultra-hard decision for you."

"It has!" Venice said. "But I really think we can find an outfit that works for all three of us."

"What?" I asked. Because in my mind, she'd already broken up with Leo. Why would she want him to be part of the costume?

"We'll have way more fun going as three anyway," Venice said. "Between Leo's jokes and your funny comments we'll be laughing nonstop."

"I'll actually be working," I said. "I'm taking pictures.

You're helping me, remember? I can't be laughing nonstop—all the pictures will turn out blurry."

"You know what I mean," Venice said. "We'll just have a better time if we're together. Do you care if I pop Leo and tell him you want to be in a costume with us?"

I crawled from my floor onto my desk chair. My emotions were whipping around inside me at lightning speed. Because for one second I had thought Leo might no longer be a part of my life and I was thrilled. But now I was planning a Halloween costume with him. Venice didn't even wait for me to respond. She tapped away on her phone with a huge smile.

"I feel so much better," she said. "What a great talk."

I heard Mitten Man scratching on my door to get inside.

"Do you mind if I let him in?" I asked. Unlike Venice, who never checked with me about anything anymore, I was still a polite friend.

"He doesn't have gas tonight, right?" Venice asked, making her stinky face.

"It was only that one time," I said defensively. "He ate something weird in the kitchen trash."

Venice continued to tap on her phone. "Sure, then. Okay," she said with a shrug.

I opened the door to let him in, and noticed my parents in a heated discussion at the kitchen table. I worried it was about the Visa bill. Apparently, my mom had bought an expensive decluttering system for the garage. Which seemed like a rotten idea. Because if we wanted to spend a bunch of money on a system, we shouldn't put it in such a lousy place.

"Don't eavesdrop," my mother said, shooting me a stern look. I slammed the door shut.

When I turned back around I saw that Venice was still popping with Leo. It was insane. My talk. My tears. They hadn't solved anything. She tried talking to me, but she was totally distracted on her phone.

"So when are you getting PopRat again?" she asked.

I rolled my eyes. It was like she wasn't paying attention to anything important in my life at all.

"I have to wait for Piper to come and give me and my parents a tutorial. I can't get PopRat until they do, remember? My mom wants to be in my sewer."

That snapped Venice back to attention. "I would die if my mom got into my sewer."

"Don't say that," I said. I was excited to be popping at all. I didn't want to think of the downside of it yet.

"Leo just sent me the funniest picture of his neighbor's cow," Venice said, laughing. "Guinea pig filter. Look."

I didn't want to look, but I did. And it was pretty hilarious. Which made me mad.

"So you're waiting for Piper?" Venice asked. "She flakes so much since she started dating Bobby. You might have to wait a month."

It bugged me that Venice was criticizing my sister. So I stood up for her. "Yeah, boyfriends are terrible and change the people I love into completely different people."

Venice got my message and put her phone away. "Okay. I'm done. Hey, what if I taught you and your parents how to PopRat?"

"Um," I said, "don't we need to work on our report?"

"Yeah, but deep, muddy-bottomed lakes are boring and PopRat is fun. Let's go ask your parents!"

Venice hopped up and zoomed out of my room.

"Dr. and Mrs. Hall," Venice said, standing at the kitchen table, "I really want to pop with Perry. And she's been waiting forever for Piper to show you how to do it. Can I show you guys? Would that be okay? It's super easy. As long as you remember your phone codes, we shouldn't have a problem."

It was pretty obvious to me that neither of my parents was interested at that exact moment in downloading PopRat and learning how to use it. But Venice didn't let up.

"We're pretty busy," my mom said, tapping on the checkbook.

"Look at this," Venice said. She lifted her phone and showed them the guinea-pigged cow. "It's hilarious, right? Perry would make the funniest pops. Can you imagine?"

Leo hadn't just made Venice a terrible friend. He'd also turned her into a terrible listener. My parents had said they were busy.

"That is pretty funny," my dad said, leaning in closer to inspect the cow. "Maybe we could use the break."

My mother sighed and rubbed her eyes.

"I'll make it fun," Venice said. "I promise it will be quick."

And poof. It happened. Venice helped us download PopRat.

"Okay," she said. "You'll need to pick your usernames and then we'll sync your address books for contacts. Or you can add them one by one, which I don't recommend. Total nightmare waste of time."

My mother looked at Venice when she said that. "I'm sure most of my contacts aren't on PopRat," she said.

"Mrs. Hall, I think you'll be surprised."

I picked PhotoKilla, which my parents objected to initially, but then agreed to after Venice convinced them it sounded strong and offered me a bunch of anonymity.

"I'm BlabBlab1 and Leo is BlabBlab2," Venice said like it was no big deal.

Really, it was pretty crushing that they were matching their usernames. Because those things lasted forever. Once you picked it, you couldn't change it. I'd read it myself in the PopRat Frequently Asked Questions page. My mother decided to use her middle name and add something she thought was hip: Mindy4Real. And my dad went full-on dentist: DrFang.

"And you both want to be added to PhotoKilla's sewer, right?" Venice asked.

"I'd prefer we referred to her as Perry in real life," my mom said.

"Right," Venice said, tapping away.

"Add me to her nest, not her sewer," my dad said.

I was bummed he'd remembered that. It made me nervous to think that my parents would be seeing every single incoming pop. It was like they didn't trust me at all.

"So it looks like you've added thirty-four contacts," Venice told my mom. "And you've added fifty-eight," she told my dad. "And you've added one hundred and nine."

"What?" my mother asked with a gasp.

"Because of her job at school she's got a metric ton of contacts," Venice said.

"How many do you have?" my mom asked her.

"Over two hundred," Venice said. "But I've been popping for a month. And almost none of those contacts are in my sewer or my nest. They're just contacts. Make sense?"

My parents both nodded. Then Venice slowly led them through sending their first pops to each other. And then to me.

"Please keep it simple," I said. "I'm either putting it in my nest or my sewer. People might see these."

Mindy4Real

Hi, Perry. Good luck with your report

DrFang

Send a Mitten Man guinea pig pic my way

After my phone buzzed and I saw the messages I just stared at them.

"You have to put them somewhere," Venice said.

I quickly swiped them both into my sewer.

"And they just stay in there forever?" my mom asked.

"You can flush them after twelve hours. But you only get two flushes a week," Venice said.

"Why?" my dad asked.

"Probably so people don't overflush and get rid of posts before people in your sewer get a chance to read them. Less flushing is better for your community."

I felt myself yawning. PopRat had lots of layers.

"See," my dad said, gesturing with his phone toward my mom, "this will be useful for us. We'll pop instead of text."

"Yeah, barring my need to send you pictures of people and

objects behaving like guinea pigs, I don't see this replacing texting for me at all," my mom said.

"I bet you get addicted!" Venice said cheerfully.

My mom looked disgusted by that comment. "Doubtful," she said.

"It's late," my dad said. "Have you two made headway on your project?"

"Some," I said, trying not to think about all the research I still had to do. When I'd picked the lake I thought researching a secret submarine-testing area would be fun. But there were way fewer articles about it than other things, like potatoes, which weren't secret and were globally loved and devoured.

"You've got to get up early for your skating adventure tomorrow," my mom said.

"It's going to be such a blast!" Venice said.

Didn't Venice get tired anymore? It was like having a boyfriend had changed her into somebody who was always excited and didn't require sleep.

"Get a good night's sleep, PhotoKilla," my dad said.

"She's Perry at home," my mom corrected.

"Night, Mrs. Hall. Night, Dr. Fang," Venice said, giggling. "Sorry. I couldn't help myself. 'Dr. Fang' is hilarious."

Venice kept giggling all the way to my room. I got a little bit excited when I felt my phone buzz, until I realized it was just her sending me crazy pops.

"I need to brush my teeth," I said. I kept hearing my phone buzz, but I was too nervous to bring it near the sink and look at it. I didn't want to accidentally drop it in water. Finally, my life had PopRat in it. I was connected. And I had 109 contacts to prove it. My life had turned a corner and I wasn't going to risk ruining it.

15

Crazy Skates

I woke up super early, even before Mitten Man, even before the sun rose. All I kept thinking about was Drea and Hayes. Just like I'd been more honest with Venice, I felt like I needed to be more honest with both of them. They couldn't just keep showing up in my life wherever and whenever they wanted. They were bumming me out in a serious way. While Venice was still sleeping, I crawled out of bed. At five o'clock in the morning, I did something I should have done weeks ago. I got out my phone and sent Drea and Hayes some super-sincere pops.

I scrolled through my contacts. Drea had picked a terrible username: HotdogGrl. For somebody trying to shed an embarrassing Internet puking experience, she seemed pretty okay reminding the world about it every time she popped. As I typed out my message, I wasn't sure I could say everything that I needed to in one pop. But I tried.

> Drea! Don't wanna sound harsh. Really wanted to help you. But you turned into a pest. Sorry

After I sent it, I realized that pop felt a little bit rude. And it also didn't really say everything I meant to say. So I tried again.

> Pest is wrong word. Sorry. But can you please stop bugging me AND my sister? We're busy. Also the fro-yo picture turned out great. So let's call this project over, okay? Great. Bye!

Two pops and my Drea problem was done. Over. Fixed. I couldn't believe how easy it was to solve it. And I'd solved it for Piper too. Sure, Piper hadn't complained about her yet, but eventually that would've happened. Drea had a problematic personality. She was way too forward and needy. I glanced over at Venice, but she was still sleeping. So I turned my attention to Hayes.

I didn't really understand his username: HACanoe. But I wrote to him anyway. Because I didn't need to have a crush. I really didn't. And I was going to tell him that as politely as I could.

> Hi, Hayes. I should have told you this sooner. I don't like you. It makes me feel weird when you give me things so you should probably give them to somebody else. Sorry

Just like after I sent Drea her first pop, I got worried that maybe I'd been too harsh, or said what I meant to say wrong. So I sent Hayes another pop really quickly.

PhotoKilla

Don't want to make you feel bad. Just trying to help you move to your next crush. Coconut balls were yummy. But I feel guilty taking them. So please give them to new crush. K? Bye!

Sending those pops made me feel a tiny bit anxious. Because I wasn't sure I'd said things the right way to Hayes. I really truly didn't want to hurt his feelings. But I also didn't want to deal with him anymore. It would have been okay if he'd crushed on me from a distance, but his trip to Fro-yo Unicorn had been the last straw, even if Javier had invited him. Then a great idea struck me. Just in case Hayes read my pops and decided to call me, I needed to give his number a special ringtone so I knew to never answer his calls. And the perfect song jumped into my head. It was a song Piper sang in the car at red lights: "Stressed Out" by Twenty-One Pilots. The lyrics didn't make much sense to me, but the beat felt perfect.

Then I thought about sending pops to Javier too, letting him know I was sick of his tasks, but I was suddenly feeling sleepy again. And I had so much skating to do in a few hours. I figured I could write that one later. So I closed my eyes and the next thing I knew, Venice was gently shaking my shoulder.

"We need to get ready," she said. "We have to pick out our outfits. Zipper-braid my hair. And eat breakfast and it's almost ten."

Our lives were so jam-packed. So we hurried as fast as we could, and even though I had watched four tutorials, zipper-braiding Venice's hair was only a partial success.

"It feels really loose," she said as we sat in the backseat of my dad's Camry.

"It doesn't look loose," I said. Even though some of the bottom loops did seem a little unsecured.

It was rare that both my mom and dad drove me someplace together, let alone Venice, but that was exactly what happened that day.

"We'll be browsing at the bookstore," my dad said. "Pop us when you're done."

"You actually don't pop people," Venice corrected. "You send pops."

"However you want to say it," my dad said. "Transmit us pops when you're finished."

"Right," I said. I liked that my ride wasn't going to be too far away. Considering everyone who was going to the rink, it was nice to think that I could flee the scene whenever I wanted.

"Venice, if you need a lift we can do that too," my mom said.

She climbed out of the car and smiled. "Thanks, but I'm set." Then she spotted Leo and screamed. *"Leo!"*

I watched her run to him as he stood leaning against the bright-blue rectangular building. I climbed out of the car too and stood beside my dad's rolled-down window.

"I'm sure they've got their transportation all figured out already. Couples are like that," I said.

My dad shook his head. "I can't believe Venice has a boy-friend." Then he gave me a concerned look, like he was asking me with his eyes to never get a boyfriend.

"I don't even like anybody right now," I told him.

He broke into a small smile. "Have a good time."

"And don't get stunty," my mom said. "I want you to come home unbroken."

"Don't worry," I said as I waved goodbye. It was like my mom didn't know me at all sometimes. I had no desire to engage in risky, bone-breaking behavior at a skating rink.

When I walked inside I felt a little bit nervous about crossing paths with Hayes. Luckily, I didn't see him around. Venice and Leo had already put on their skates and they rushed right over to where I was renting mine.

"Did you see that Hayes gave us free snack coupons?" Venice asked. "He's so awesome."

That was actually really nice of him. I glanced around.

"I don't see him," I said.

"Yeah," Leo said. "Nobody has."

That made me feel a tiny bit more nervous. And if Leo hadn't been standing right there, I might have told Venice about the pops I'd sent Hayes while she was sleeping. But I just didn't feel comfortable talking about my personal life in front of Leo. Maybe when he went to the bathroom I'd tell Venice. Or maybe I'd pop her about it later.

I looked out onto the skating rink and saw a really tall guy Rollerblading like a fiend. He was wearing a helmet, so I couldn't tell who it was, but based on the well-defined biceps it sort of looked like Victor, Venice's brother. He centered himself on the ramp and launched his whole body several feet into the air.

"Wow," I said. "I'd break my neck if I tried that."

"Victor is very talented," Leo said. "He's good at everything."

Before I could agree, I saw Anya skate by with Sabrina and Sailor. They looked like they were having such a good time. I wondered what they were all thinking about. Didn't they have any stress in their lives? They sure didn't seem to. Maybe when they put on roller skates, it all melted away.

I took my skates to a bench and slipped off my shoes. Instead of rolling onto the rink, Venice took a seat next to me on the bench. Tragically, Leo stood beside her.

"So Leo and I want to talk to you about something," Venice said.

I felt myself breathe a little faster. Were they about to lay some bad news on me? It sure sounded like that. Which seemed double awful, because there were two of them and one of me.

"What is it?" I asked. I tried to breathe normally.

"We think we've figured out our group costume," Venice said, reaching down and squeezing my hand. "And it's something super amazing."

"What?" I said. Because I thought I should be involved in the planning stage and not just have the costume sprung on me.

"Curious George and the Man with the Yellow Hat won't work for three people," Venice said.

"Right," I said. Not only that, but it was a terrible idea for a costume anyway.

"Mr. Falconer gives extra credit if you go as something

Idaho-themed," Leo said. His eyes looked wide and happy, like he thought his ideas were amazing.

"Don't worry," Venice said. "We've already ruled out Lewis and Clark. It's a two-person costume. But what if we went as miners?"

"What?" I asked. Because it sounded like Venice had said "miners."

Leo shoved his phone in my face. "Like these guys. They already look like they're wearing costumes."

"And no fur!" Venice said. "Isn't it the perfect costume idea? Leo thought of it last night in his sleep. He woke up and *boom*. There it was."

Leo was smiling huge, like he was the smartest person to ever wear skates and stand beside a bench.

"I don't want to dress up like a dude," I said. "Even for extra credit."

Venice seemed shocked to hear this. "Getting extra credit would take some of the pressure off our report."

I stood my ground. "Do you know how hot we'd get wearing mining hats all day? We'd probably all get headaches."

And because Venice understood that I would never in a million years dress up as a miner, she said, "Okay. Fine. Do you have any ideas?"

I tried really hard to think of something clever. "Piper and a couple of friends wore giant cardboard squares around their heads and went as selfies."

Leo looked disappointed by that suggestion. "That was hot two years ago. It would be stale to do it now."

I couldn't believe Leo called my suggestion stale. It was like he was daring me to hate him.

"We could go as a BLT sandwich," Leo said.

"Gross," I said. "My sister is a vegan. I refuse to dress like a meat product."

"You could go as the L or the T," Leo said in a snarky way.

"Not happening," I said. I started to lace up my skates. I felt like it was suddenly my job to come up with an idea for the perfect three-person costume. It was so much pressure.

"Robots would work," Leo said.

That idea sounded difficult. I needed full use of my arms and peripheral vision. I tried to think of a kind way to turn that idea down. "Wearing a box to school would suck."

"Three-person costumes are so hard," Venice said.

"Well, we don't have to think of it right now," Leo said. "We could skate."

And before we could all agree with that, Victor came speeding up and brilliantly pivoted and stopped right in front of us.

"Is this the chatting bench?" he asked. "Is this where everybody goes to talk?"

"Hi, Victor," I said. "I like your moves."

"I'm trying," Victor said, flashing me an awesome smile.

"We're getting ready to go skate now," I said.

"We were trying to figure out our Halloween costumes," Venice said. "We're trying to think of something for the three of us."

"That's easy," Victor said. "A three-humped camel."

Venice frowned. "We don't want to be attached. We have different classes."

"Okay," Victor said. "There are a trillion ideas. Pirates, fairies, zombies, the Beastie Boys."

"Perry won't dress like a dude," Venice said in a really judgmental way.

"That's cool," Victor said. "You gotta do what feels right."

I watched as he weaved through the crowd and then wiggled and fishtailed. He was so athletic. It blew my mind.

"I don't want to go as fairies. I'm allergic to glitter," Leo said.

"I don't want to go as a pirate or a zombie," Venice said.

"Who are the Beastie Boys?" I asked.

Leo shrugged. "Hey, do you wanna get snacks?"

"Totally," Venice said, grabbing his hand.

"Okay," I said, standing up onto my skates and catching my balance, and moving toward the snack line. "I wonder if Hayes is working at the counter." Because sometimes he helped make the nachos.

"Oh," a voice said behind me. "He's not coming."

I turned to see who was talking. Anya. I should have known. I turned back around and lost my balance a little. I had to grab on to a metal pole or I would've hit the floor.

"Is he doing homework?" Leo asked.

"Nope," Anya said. "He told me somebody sent him some crappy pops and he wasn't coming."

I kept holding on to the pole so I didn't fall down. Everything felt very unsteady all of a sudden.

"Who would send Hayes crappy pops?" Venice asked. "That's awful."

"He didn't say," Anya said. "But it's lame. Hayes is totally nice."

I couldn't believe that Anya was judging me, even though she didn't know she was judging me. It sucked.

"What can I get you guys?" the counter clerk asked. He was young and had acne and had scabby elbows just like Hayes. I stayed silent while Venice and Leo ordered a smorgasbord of snacks. "And for you?" the clerk asked.

I felt so terrible. I stood and stared at the menu items. Then I ordered what I felt I deserved. "I'll just take a cup of ice."

"Ooh, too bad, so sad, but the ice machine is broken," the clerk said.

"That's okay," I said. "I don't need anything."

I looked around and realized I didn't see Drea either. Maybe my pops had been tougher than I'd meant them to be.

"You can share what we got," Venice said. "You need to eat something."

But I didn't think that was true. I felt really guilty. And it didn't feel right to be using Hayes's gifts anymore.

"I'm not feeling so hot," I said. "I'm going to send my mom a pop."

"Wait," Venice said.

But I didn't wait. I skated back toward the bench with my shoes. I couldn't stay here. I didn't deserve to be at a roller rink having fun. Besides, I needed to work anyway. I couldn't remember what specific tasks I had to do to get ready for class portraits, but I knew I had a bunch of them. And they weren't going to complete themselves.

16

Floating Heads

Before the day even started, I knew it was going to be weird. Because for Venice and me to take class portraits, we had to spend all day in the back corner of the cafeteria taking photos. We wouldn't be going to our classes. And it was our job to tell everybody what to do. I had mixed feelings about this.

As I walked to school, Venice popped me a photo of Chet Baez. I sent her a return pop.

PhotoKilla
> Why Chet pic?

It seemed weird to send me a random photo from the bus. I suspected there was some extra meaning that I was missing.

BlabBlab1
> He's not wearing feathers! Looks good. Nerds took our advice. Penny Moffett and Poppy Lansing look cute too. YAY!! 😭

That made me feel a little bit relieved. Chet wore feathers all the time. And for him, a feather-free photo was the first step in taking a portrait that looked decent. I smiled. I really did want everybody's portrait to turn out. I felt like it was the least I could do for all the kids at my school, especially the geeky ones. My phone buzzed again and it was a pop from Leo. Gag.

BlabBlab2

We could go as wilderness surveyors?

Then he sent me a photo of a trio of weird-looking bearded dudes wearing backpacks and carrying photography equipment up a mountain. Leo didn't know me at all. Going to school dressed like a bearded mountain climber was the last thing I wanted to do. So I sent him a pop explaining this.

PhotoKilla

NOT GOING AS A DUDE!

And then it was like Leo couldn't stop himself from being annoying, because he sent me another pop.

BlabBlab2

Women R surveyors too

Leo sent me an old-timey photo of a woman in a weird hat carrying a long pole and standing beside a bunch of trees. I bet we weren't allowed to bring poles to school, even on Halloween. What was wrong with Leo? I didn't need extra credit in Idaho History this badly. Seriously. This needed to stop.

Already have costume. You 2 do you 2. I'll do me

Then I made sure that I'd swiped all my incoming pops into my sewer and kept walking to school. When I was a street away I noticed somebody in front of me wearing an orange T-shirt. For four seconds, I stopped breathing. I thought for sure it was Hayes. But then I realized it was just some random seventh grader who'd worn an orange T-shirt to school. It was hard to relax, knowing that Hayes and Drea were out there. And that eventually our paths would cross. Nobody missed portrait day. Nobody.

When I walked through the halls I kept my head down and my eyes glued to my phone. I'd been trying to get some advice from Piper about the pops I'd sent to Drea and Hayes. But she hadn't returned any of my pops. I was beginning to worry that she'd already gone to Thailand with Bobby. But then I wondered if she had a new PopRat account.

I'd been sending everything to Piperathon, because that was the contact that came up on my phone. But I was pretty sure she'd probably discontinued that username because it didn't reflect who she was anymore. That was Piper before college. Not now. I was pretty sure Piper had stopped running after she found yoga and Bobby.

When I got to the Yearbook room without having any disastrous run-ins, I felt like I'd reached a safe place. But then I opened the door and found a horde of eighth graders primping with Anya, and my safe place felt suddenly dangerous.

"Don't interrupt me," Anya said. "I'm giving Reece cat eyes."

I did a double take. Because Anya was not giving Reece subtle and attractive cat eyes, she was applying goopy black eyeliner all over her face.

"Have you shown her what it looks like?" I asked. Because it was going to take a ton of water and gentle scrubbing to get that crud off Reece's face before I took her picture.

"Um, yes," Anya said in a snotty voice, flipping around. "They look like mine."

I gasped. Anya's eyes looked like horrible cartoon eyes. They were rimmed in thick black lines and had weird dark triangles in their corners. Then I gasped again. Because clearly they'd forgotten that today was portrait day and they were practicing Halloween costumes and now their faces didn't look normal and eighth-grade portraits started in ten minutes.

"Crap!" I yelled. "You've forgotten about portraits. You need to get that gunk off your eyes."

Reece laughed. And so did Sabrina and Sailor. And that was when I heard a boy's laugh. It was Fletcher Zamora. His eyes looked awful too.

"We've done this specifically for portraits," Anya said. "It's going to look hilarious and cool."

I blinked. I agreed that it looked hilarious, but it certainly didn't look cool.

"I bet Principal Hunt will make you wash it off," I said. Because it seemed wrong to make yourself look purposely weird for the yearbook. Those books belonged to everybody. I wanted my picture of Anya to look like Anya. Not a lynx with eye funk.

"Wrong. Principal Hunt is cool with it," Anya said.

"Yeah," Fletcher said. "Eighth graders always make their mark."

Ugh. It was disgusting. Anya had figured out a way to hijack the portraits. It really bugged me. It was hard to accept what was happening. I just kept staring at them.

"You should get the camera and head to the cafeteria," Anya said. "Setup always takes more time than you think."

It was at this exact moment that I started to wonder if working on the yearbook was worth all this stress. Was it making me happy? Not really. Was it hurting my performance in other classes? Yeah. Was it wrecking my social life? I was pretty sure that it was. But I didn't have a lot of time to sort out my feelings about it. Because Anya was right: Setups did take a ton of time. I grabbed the camera and headed down the hall. Again, because I felt incredibly nervous about running into Hayes and Drea, I pulled my phone out, and instead of popping, I started straight-up texting Piper.

Me

I need you. I sent terrible pops to people who hate me now 😭

Me

I've made a million mistakes. Help! 😭 😭

Me

After school, will try to get a cab to take me to your school. Must see you 😭 😭 😭 😭 😭 😭 😭 😭 😭 😭

That last one caught her attention.

Chill. In class. Taking test. Talk later

It was such a relief to see that text from Piper, even though it didn't help me at all. I was still staring at my phone when I felt somebody bump my shoulder. I panicked and dropped my phone. I watched it bounce down the cafeteria steps.

"I'm so sorry!" Venice gushed. "I didn't mean to bump you that hard."

I hurried down the stairs and picked up my phone. It had tumbled down three stairs and landed flat on its face on the hard tiled floor. I thought for sure my whole screen had broken into a web of cracks. But when I picked it up and flipped it over it was perfectly fine. When Venice saw this she hugged me.

"I'm crazy sorry," she said.

And I couldn't get super mad at her, because I was pretty sure I'd dropped it out of fear. I didn't think she'd actually bumped it out of my hand.

"Have you seen Hayes?" I asked.

Venice did the most horrible thing ever when I asked her that question. She looked away and mumbled, "Not really."

That was weird. Because either you've seen somebody or you haven't seen somebody. It wasn't really possible to "not really" see somebody.

"Why are you acting weird about Hayes?" I asked. Because I strongly suspected that something was up.

"I'm not. Why are *you* acting weird about Hayes?" she asked.

And that was when I confessed. Because I needed some

help. I couldn't handle this problem on my own. "I sent him mean pops. I'm the one who made him skip skating."

And then Venice said the worst thing ever: "Yeah. I know."

"What?" I asked. Because it meant she'd been keeping important information from me.

Venice sighed and pulled out her phone. "Both Drea and Hayes forwarded them to my sewer."

And I didn't even know that could happen.

"When?" I asked.

"Last night," Venice said, scrolling through her phone to show me.

"Don't. Don't," I said, shielding my eyes. "I don't want to remind myself of what I said."

I moved one of my fingers so I could look at her. Her face was filled with sympathy. "There's nothing you can do about it now. They're out there."

And the way she said that made it seem like my pops were escaped dogs or something. Running around doing anything they wanted. Venice could tell I was totally freaked out, because she slipped off her backpack, unzipped it, and offered me a chocolate bar.

"I brought these for later. To give us extra energy. But maybe you should just eat yours now," Venice said.

I took the bar and tore off the wrapper. "Do you think they hate me?" I asked. "I don't want anybody to hate me."

"They *probably* don't *hate* you," Venice said.

But she didn't say it with much confidence.

"Besides, you wanted Hayes to stop crushing on you. And you wanted Drea to back off. Now you've pushed them out of your life forever. Problem solved, right?"

"Um, forever?" I said. Because I hadn't meant to do *that*.

"Glad to see you've got the camera," Ms. Kenny said as she walked over to us. "Let's take some test shots in front of the screen."

Ms. Kenny had a huge projector screen rolled up under her arm. And Principal Hunt was carrying a couple of bags. And Javier popped up out of nowhere, drinking out of a thermos.

"The back corner we used last year worked really well," Principal Hunt said. "Great light, no shadows, and students can form a line along the wall."

I followed behind everybody as we made our way to the corner. The strong smell of spicy beef hovered over us.

"Looks like they're serving walking tacos for lunch," Javier said.

Javier was always pointing out stuff that either didn't matter at all or was totally obvious. And it was as if I was the only person who was annoyed by this.

"Do we get to eat lunch?" Venice asked.

I'd just assumed that we would get to eat lunch. There was a chance we might not eat lunch?

"Absolutely," Ms. Kenny said. "It's customary for the photography crew to eat pizza with me back in the Yearbook room during lunch while we regroup and prepare for the second round."

"Does that include Anya?" I asked. I thought I'd only been thinking that question. But then I heard myself saying it.

"Yes. The whole crew," Ms. Kenny said.

Principal Hunt gave me a quick look and then pulled out a list. "Does this look like the order I should gather the rooms, Ms. Kenny?"

"Perfect," Ms. Kenny replied. "We can take one room every twenty minutes."

One class every twenty minutes? Wow. This was going to be a ton of work. We probably should've scheduled different grades for different days.

"And some of the students are dressing outlandishly," Principal Hunt said. "I gave permission for some of it, but a few people are really pushing the limit. If you think anything is in poor taste, point it out. Student portraits are a privilege. I'm not letting anything crazy in the yearbook."

And I sort of wondered if this meant we could refuse to take Anya's photo.

When the first bell rang and Ms. Kenny led the first class to us, I was totally crushed by what I saw. Yes, Fletcher and Reece had cat eyes, but it was worse than that. Four members of the boys' basketball team had worn cream-colored sweaters. Against the screen, they were going to look like floating heads. And this wasn't an accident. A bunch of kids had dressed in that color. I was stunned. It was like they were using my photo-clinic tips to purposely take a bad picture. It was so rude. My life had so much stress in it, and here these goons were, totally wasting my time and my talent.

"Hi, Perry," Tate Lloyd said, flashing me a hideously gummy smile. Okay. I got it. All these popular kids wanted to show up and take terrible yearbook photos. Fine. No problem. I was here to do my job. And I was going to do it. No matter how horrendous these jerks looked.

"The nerds look great," Venice said.

And she was right. Everybody who'd taken our advice looked way better than they would've otherwise. *But the rest of them.* The rest of them. Let's just say in addition to the cat eyes and floating heads, there was a lot of unblended pimple cream happening. At one point, I couldn't take it anymore and told Ms. Kenny, "I feel a little mocked."

She put a hand on my shoulder. "You're doing a fantastic job."

But that compliment didn't make me feel any less mocked.

"It'll be okay. Don't panic. Here come Drea and Hayes," Venice whispered to me while I took Nicole Salazar's photo.

And that was my first hint that things might not be okay. I saw Drea before I saw Hayes. I couldn't believe they were in the same class. But there they were, standing in a clump of kids from Ms. Stott's class. They looked good. They hadn't done anything to sabotage their appearance. Drea sat on the stool first.

"Hi," I said, trying to sound totally normal.

"Hi, Perry," Drea said.

She was quick about it. It definitely sounded like she was upset with me. But I wasn't sure if she hated me. I tried to ignore that she was wearing one of Piper's old shirts and a pair of her leggings.

"It turned out great!" I said really cheerfully after I took Drea's picture.

She shrugged. "It's just a picture."

And that was a bigger slam than anybody realized. Because she knew that I'd been trying extra hard to get a good picture of her into the yearbook. And she knew how I felt about my photos. Every single one of them mattered.

Next up was Hayes. I was so nervous that I didn't even say anything to him. And he didn't say anything to me. I took his picture, and he was gone. I didn't even have time to look out from around the camera. By the time I did, it was just the empty chair. Venice leaned in close to my ear.

"Don't read too much into their hate faces or their hate shirts," she whispered.

I wasn't sure what that meant. Because I hadn't even noticed those. But there they were. On the back of both their shirts, written in bright-red marker: NO LOVE 4 HATERS.

Wow. I felt like I'd been punched in the face. Nobody had ever worn clothes in order to send me a message before. Plus, it sort of stung to see that Drea had defaced one of Piper's shirts.

"That might not be about me, right?" I asked.

"Well," Venice said, "you really hurt their feelings. Maybe you should apologize."

But I wasn't sure I knew how to do that. Because that would mean having to explain my pops and rehash my feelings about Hayes's crush on me and Drea's sister-stealing behavior, and I felt the better solution was not to say anything and let time fix that stuff.

"I think I'm just going to give them space," I said. "I mean, I'm sure they'll mellow."

And when I watched them walk away that day in their matching hate shirts, I really did believe things would return to normal fairly quickly. Big Boo was almost here. Oral reports were almost due. We had so many other things to be doing. We had so much other stuff to worry about.

17

Filtered

I must have figured something magical would happen and that I would stumble into the perfect Halloween costume. Literally. Which was why I'd agreed to enter the garage with my mother and spend an hour going through the plastic bins. Because maybe one of Piper's old costumes was out there, just waiting for me to find it.

My mother understood what I was after. "If you don't find something here, you can always go as a cat. You look so cute with whiskers."

I pictured Anya and her gang of friends and their horrendous cat eyes that I had forever immortalized in the yearbook.

"I can't go as a cat this year," I said. "It's just not possible."

Mitten Man found a piece of paper and chased it around the concrete floor, skittering into boxes.

"Ghosts are easy," my mom said. "You could use this sheet."

She pulled out an old bedsheet from the dryer. It had a big stain on it, right where my head would be.

"Do you know how terrible my life would be at school if I dressed like a ghost with a brown stain?"

My mom must have gone to the nicest middle school ever, because she didn't seem to understand how urgent finding an amazing costume was to me. I kept pulling things out of the bin and setting them in piles. Tragically, the piles were a little wobbly.

"You're making a mess of Piper's things," my mom said. "We need to keep some order."

But keeping order took time and I didn't have any of that to spare.

"Didn't she go as a jellyfish?" I asked. "Didn't she win a prize for that?"

"We don't have that costume anymore. It involved balloons and rubber tubing and you were obsessed with it and we worried it was a suffocation risk."

But that didn't make sense, because I was five when Piper wore that costume. "How would I suffocate myself? That's stupid."

My mom put her hand on her hip and spoke really harshly to me. "You kept biting the balloons. It was a legitimate concern. Not a stupid one."

"Sorry," I said. Because I didn't want my mom to get upset with me. I dug to the very bottom of bin number one and set it aside. But when I reached for bin number two my mom stopped me.

"What about all those piles you made?" she asked.

Card stock, construction paper, pipe cleaners, glitter, cotton balls, crepe paper. I watched them swaying under the weight of their own terrible height.

"They'll be fine," I said.

Whoosh. When all the artwork crashed to the floor I felt truly bad for Piper's stuff. Especially because some of the pieces lost their cotton balls.

"You're done," my mom said. "All you're doing is wreaking havoc."

"But I need a costume for tomorrow!" I said.

"Why do you do this to yourself?" she asked. "Why would you put something so important off to the last minute?"

And that seemed like a horrible thing to tell me while I was panicking. Because how I had gotten into this terrible situation didn't matter at all. The only thing I needed was a solution.

"Be a cat," my mom said. "That's my best advice."

I stood there for a few seconds waiting for some better advice, but she didn't give me any.

"Piper has been acting weird and won't return my texts," I said. "She won't even respond to me on PopRat. Maybe you can call her and make her call me back."

"Perry!" my mom said in a really grumpy voice. "It's not your sister's job to solve your problems. You need to lay off the texts and pops. You'll drive her away."

And that was probably the worst thing my mother had ever said to me. And instead of trying to get her to take it back, I hurried into the house and turned on my computer. Because if my mom and sister couldn't help me solve my problems, I really only had one place left to turn: the Internet.

I found it lame how many blogs suggested witches, mermaids, and princesses. None of those things appealed to me.

They looked complicated and involved hats or tails or crowns. If I could go as anything, I wanted to go as an animal. But I didn't want to go as a funny animal, like a cow or a pig. And I didn't want to go as a large animal, like a hippo or an elephant. It was just so hard.

Knock. Knock. Knock.

I was pretty sure my mom was knocking on my door until I heard, "It's Dad. Can I come in?"

And even though I needed to stay focused on searching the web, I said, "Okay. But I'm pretty busy."

My dad opened the door and held his arms out wide like he wanted to hug me. Which bugged me, because I'd just told him I was pretty busy.

"Do you want any help?" he asked.

"No," I said in a mopey voice. I clicked on a website that offered patterns to make buccaneer costumes. Never. *Click.*

"I understand what you're going through," my dad said. "In grad school my department used to have the biggest Halloween party and everybody wore amazing and mind-blowing costumes. I still have pictures."

I frowned at him. I didn't think I had time to make one of those. "I don't need something amazing. I need something clever, quick, and easy. Something that won't stick out."

"I've got it," he said. "Go as a selfie."

I couldn't believe he was suggesting Piper's costume from two years ago. "I need something more original."

"Let's stay in that lane," my dad said, tapping his chin. "Phone culture. What's popular right now? PopRat. And what's popular there?"

I really didn't want to talk about PopRat with my dad. I was sort of thinking PopRat might have been a mistake, because it definitely wasn't improving my life yet.

"Photo filters," he went on. "Go as a hamster lens."

And I was all ready to reject this idea and tell my dad it was totally stupid, but it was actually pretty good.

"It's a guinea pig that's popular right now," I corrected.

"Then go as a guinea pig filter," he said.

"But I'll need to wear a frame, right? Or I'll just look like a guinea pig and not a guinea pig lens, right?"

"We've got an old box in the garage. I can make you a frame. And I know you've got to take pictures at the carnival, so I'll make it so you can set it down."

"Wow," I said.

"Wow what?" my dad asked.

"Normally it's really hard to solve my problems. This was easy."

"Remember this, Perry Hall. Two heads are always better than one. And your dad has a pretty decent head." He pointed at me and said, "Bada bing."

Which sort of killed the mood. Because "bada bing" was a lame thing to say.

After my dad informed my mom of my costume idea, we worked as a team to make it. For ears my mom found great fabric scraps that she attached to a headband with her glue gun. My dad made me the perfect frame from an old air-conditioner box that he even branded with the PopRat logo. And I found a great online makeup tutorial that taught me how to play up my guinea pig features, which I didn't even know I had.

"Try these on," my mom said, handing me gray mittens with the fingertips cut off. She'd glued on fluffy fur and converted them into the perfect pair of guinea pig paws.

I slid them on and the finished product was actually quite good.

"You should send a picture of this to Piper," my dad said.

But I just frowned when he said that. Because Piper was basically ghosting me.

Just then, my phone buzzed. I got a little bit excited because I thought maybe it was Piper. But it was Venice.

"Is that a picture?" my dad asked, leaning in and invading my space.

It figured that she had finished her costume at the same exact time I'd finished mine. We were best friends. Even though I didn't feel totally in sync with her, our lives were still super connected. Then I looked at the picture and felt bummed out.

"It's Venice *and* Leo in their costumes," I said.

"Let's see," my mom said. "Ooh. Miners. I love their hats."

But I just stared at that photo and felt sorry for them. Because the dirty jackets they were wearing were monstrous. If Venice thought fur was too hot, wait until she spent the entire day wearing that canvas getup and a helmet. She'd be a puddle of sweat by lunch.

"You should send them a photo," my mom suggested, lifting up her phone to snap one.

But I jumped out of picture range and screamed, "No way!" I hid behind a chair to make sure she couldn't photograph me. "I want my costume to be a surprise."

"You're so dramatic," my mother said.

But I didn't think that was true. I was thinking ahead to tomorrow, where I wanted to make a surprising entrance in my guinea pig costume and impress my whole school.

"Let's call this a successful evening," my dad said with a yawn. "I think I'm ready for bed."

But we didn't go to bed. Because all three of our phones started buzzing.

"It's Piper," my mom said. "What's this?"

We all stared at the photo and caption Piper had sent. It was of her and Bobby. They were sitting in a café, smiling and holding up a letter. "We got accepted to teach ESL in Thailand. So thrilled. You're probably not. Turning off my phone now. Calm down and we'll talk later. Namaste."

I watched as my father's face began to turn red. "How do you finish college and go to Thailand?" he said. "She's dropping out!"

"Let's not assume the worst," my mom said.

"We should've put our foot down about Thailand when it first came up," my dad said.

"You knew about Thailand?" I asked. Because I had thought I was doing my mother and sister a favor by keeping it a secret and not talking about it in front of him.

"Of course I told your father about Thailand," my mother said. "We tell each other everything."

And that actually frightened me a little bit. Because there were certain parts of my life that I preferred only one of them know about.

"I'm going to drive down there right now and kick Bobby's butt right out of her life," my dad said.

"Wow," I said. Because my dad had never threatened to kick anybody's butt before.

"You'll make things worse," my mom said.

"Piper flunking out of college is the worst-case scenario," my dad said, looking really upset.

But I felt like it was my job to stick up for Piper. "She might not flunk all her classes. She's very smart."

"You think you're raising a normal daughter and then she meets one hipster bozo and this happens," my dad said.

"Actually, I do think boyfriends ruin people," I said, trying to stay involved with the conversation.

"Well, driving to Pocatello and forcing an encounter with Bobby isn't a good solution," my mom said. "We need to think strategically."

Then they stared at each other and didn't say anything. I wished I could have offered them a suggestion. But I didn't know how to break people up, even though lately I'd given that topic a lot of thought.

"I'm going to text Piper anyway. Maybe she hasn't turned off her phone yet," I said. I ran to the mirror and took a selfie. Then I popped it to her with the caption, "Guess what I am for Halloween?"

My mom and dad and I stared at my phone, hoping for a reply. But it never came. So we all got ready for bed. While I was brushing my teeth I heard my parents talking.

"Don't worry," my mom said. "I've tucked her passport away. She isn't going anywhere."

And that was a huge relief to hear. Because I didn't want to think of Piper in a cobra-filled country with Bobby. Even if that was what she wanted. Because it wasn't what I wanted. What I wanted wasn't complicated at all. I wanted a happy life. With my best friend. And my sister. And a great Halloween costume. And for Javier to be a better leader. And no more tasks. And to get an A on my Lake Pend Oreille presentation. And get As in all my classes. And all my Big Boo pictures to turn out. And also the thing with Drea and Hayes to be ancient history. I hardly wanted anything at all.

18

Who?

When I woke up, I was pretty thrilled to see that Piper had responded to my pop in the middle of the night. As soon as I saw it I started yelling, "She popped me back! She popped me back!"

My parents came into my bedroom still in their pajamas, looking pretty relieved.

"What did she say?" my mom asked.

"Did she mention whether or not she's still going to her classes?" my dad asked.

But I just ignored that question. Because of course Piper hadn't texted me about that. "Okay. She said, 'Hi, Perry. Love you so much. Don't worry. I'll come and give you a big hug before I go. And you look *great*, Smudge!'"

"I am not letting my firstborn go to Thailand at nineteen," my mom said. "That's final."

"I'll email her advisor," my dad said. "We can set up a meeting. Find out her academic standing."

Then he patted me on the head like I was a dog. "At least one of my daughters is keeping her head on straight."

And I really didn't like it when my parents compared me to Piper, even when it was a compliment. So I said, "Maybe Piper needs a break. Maybe going to Thailand isn't as terrible as we think." Because my sister usually made pretty good choices.

But my parents both gave me a worried look. "If she fails out of college and jets off to Thailand," my dad said, "nothing improves for anyone."

And that actually sounded like a true statement, so I just said, "Yeah." But then my mind leaped to something else that Piper had said. "Why did she call me Smudge?"

My mom shrugged. "Term of endearment?"

"Maybe she thought the picture looked smudged," my dad said as he walked out of my room.

And while neither of those answers felt right, I also wasn't too worried about the Smudge comment. Piper had a lot on her mind. Maybe it was a weird autocorrect. Or maybe it was something she meant to say to somebody else.

Walking to school carrying my PopRat frame was not the easiest thing I'd ever done in my life. It was heavy, and wobbly, and I had a tremendous fear that a gust of wind would bend it and possibly tear one of the sides. So I walked slowly and tried to carry it with the breeze, like a sail cutting through the air.

Luckily, the front doors of the school were propped open, so I didn't have to set my costume down. I heard a few people make exaggerated meowing sounds at me, which hurt my feelings. Because I was pretty sure I didn't look like a cat—I didn't have any whiskers and I had guinea pig ears. I hoped maybe they were meowing at a costume behind me. Instead of going to my locker, I glided straight to the Yearbook room. I needed to check the task sheet and possibly take some pictures before school, if I had time and Ms. Kenny said it was okay.

I was super surprised when I entered the room to see that Venice and Leo were already there, dressed head to toe as full-on miners. They looked ridiculous. But I couldn't tell them that, because Ms. Kenny was talking to them. I heard her say, "What an outrageously great costume, you two." Which meant she liked their mining getup, which felt weird to me. She usually had such good taste.

"Hi," I said, gently setting down my PopRat frame next to the whiteboard.

"Wow," Venice said. "I can't believe you pulled that costume together so quickly."

That did not feel like a compliment.

"Amazing," Leo said. "It's perfect. You nailed it."

Gag. I really didn't want Leo to be complimenting me. Because did that mean I had to fake-compliment his awful beard?

"Have you thought about adding a donation jar to your costume?" Ms. Kenny asked. "I'm sure the Humane Society would be happy to get more Smudge donations."

It was then, at the second mention of the name Smudge, that I realized I was missing something important. Mainly, who was Smudge? And was I really dressed like him/her/it? Sadly, I didn't feel like I could ask Venice, Leo, or Ms. Kenny. Because they'd already complimented my costume. So I had to figure out who Smudge was on my own. I pulled out my phone. Boom! There he was. It only took two seconds to find his whole terrible life story.

Smudge was all over the local news. Apparently, an apartment building on St. Claire Road caught fire and a bunch of families were displaced. And a stray cat, Smudge, got burned too. The pictures showed him wrapped in a towel with an IV attached to his gray paw. I looked at my own paws. The way my mom had cut the mittens did make them look a tiny bit injured. And my ears, if you didn't understand they were guinea pig ears, could look like damaged cat ears. And my face, whiskerless and painted white and tan, did strongly resemble poor, burned Smudge.

"What are you looking at?" Venice asked. "Did you get a Smudge update?"

I blinked. Why would I be getting a Smudge update? Ms. Kenny handed me an empty sour cream tub that normally held colored pencils.

"You could use this for a donation jar," she suggested.

"Leo and I can decorate it!" Venice said. "It will help with all of Smudge's medical bills."

"Sure," I said. Because it felt rude to say I didn't want to help collect money for a burned cat. Especially since everybody thought I was dressed to look like him.

"Great!" Venice said. Then she and Leo grabbed the sour cream container and headed to the craft table.

I really hated the idea of carrying my frame, my books, and a donation jar around school all day. Suddenly, it felt like my costume had too many pieces.

"Holy smokes!" Anya said the second she saw me. "You really love cats. I mean, out of all the cute costumes in the world, instead of choosing one of those, you dressed as our city's most famous and probably ugliest fire escapee, Smudge. Wow."

Sabrina and Sailor joined her and all three of them just gawked at me.

"Boom," Sailor said. "You've really blown my mind."

"Yeah," Sabrina said. "You've got guts. I always think of Halloween as the one day I get to wear a tail or glitter or a tiara. I try to look cute."

The way they looked at me made me feel really ugly, even deformed. I wanted to correct everybody and explain that I wasn't Smudge. That I was a PopRat guinea pig filter. But for some reason, those words never came out. I just stared back at them. They were dressed like ice cream cones. They had cherry hats on their heads. And beads all over their shirts that looked like rainbow sprinkles. And brown miniskirts that looked like waffle cones. Anya was vanilla, Sabrina was chocolate, and Sailor was strawberry. I was jealous. In addition to being super cute, their costumes looked easy to move in.

"Wowza!" Javier said. "I didn't see this coming. You're Smudge!"

And that basically sealed my fate. Because after seven people, eight counting your own sister, call you Smudge on Halloween, you're Smudge.

"What can I say? I love cats." And even though I hadn't meant that to be a hilarious joke, Anya, Sabrina, and Sailor burst out laughing.

After Yearbook, I had to choose between carrying my filter or my Smudge donation jar around with me. Taking both was impossible. I chose the latter. I felt weird collecting money for a cat whose existence I had only just learned about. But Ms. Kenny checked with Principal Hunt, and she assured me that I had permission to do it, as long as I turned my bucket in to her at the end of the day.

I was a magnet. Lots of kids sought me out just to ask about the fire, which I knew nothing about. Even Reece Fontaine, Hannah Jones, and Fletcher Zamora tracked me down between classes as I made my way to Science.

"I heard it was a candle," Hannah said, dressed like an amazing ninja in all black with super-tall black boots. She even wore a dramatic black mask.

I shrugged. "I really don't know the details."

"Wasn't it a propane explosion?" Fletcher asked. "Somebody brought a canister inside and it had a leak."

"Why would anybody do that?" I asked, adjusting my fake-fur mittens.

"Yeah," Reece said, giving me a friendly shoulder bump. "I didn't think it was that either."

"I hope his ears don't get infected," Hannah said, staring at my fur costume ears.

"It sounds like he's getting great medical care now," I said, repositioning my headband so my own ears didn't droop.

"You're so awesome," Reece said. Then she dumped some change into my donation jar and ran off.

It was like that all day leading up to the Big Boo. People found me, complimented my bravery in coming as a hideously injured stray cat, and threw money into my sour cream tub. *Cha-ching.* It was pretty exhausting. I wasn't sure how I'd have the energy to take pictures at the carnival. But it wasn't like I had a choice, because it was going to happen.

Instead of class, for fifth and sixth period we all got to go to the carnival in the gym. The student council, drama club, and PTA had planned and executed the whole thing: decorations, activity booths, treats, and all the extras. All we had to do was go to the gym and enjoy it. Except for me and Venice, because we had to photograph it.

I met Venice at the beginning of lunch to see if she wanted to eat in the cafeteria, or go to the Yearbook room and prep stuff.

"I need something to drink," she said.

She looked very pink.

"You should take your helmet off," I said. "It looks like you're overheating."

She pulled out a water bottle from her backpack and chugged it. "The helmet makes the costume. I'm not taking it off."

"If you get heat stroke, I'll be marooned," I pleaded. "Don't do that to me."

"I'm not gonna let you down, Smudge," Venice said, finishing her water. "Wow, how much have you made in donations?"

I shrugged. "I haven't counted it."

"You're such a giver," Venice said, giving me a quick hug. "Let's grab our stuff and head to the gym. I'm dying to see what they've done."

From what I'd heard from seventh and eighth graders, Big Boo was totally awesome and very Halloweeny. Fake pumpkins. Scarecrows. Bats. Witches. But what I saw when I entered the gymnasium was so much better than what I thought I was going to see.

The first thing that deeply impressed me was the fog machine. It pumped out a tremendous amount of cool mist that made everything feel so spooky. And then there was the background music. It was a supercreepy mix of croaking toads, haunting music, screaming people, and moaning. And I was expecting maybe twenty pumpkins, but laid out before me were at least a hundred. And they were all carved with spooky faces. They lined a pathway that led to an apple-bobbing booth. Somebody's mom dressed as a mean green witch looked to be in charge of that activity. Her warts looked very real and hairy.

"I don't even feel like I'm in school anymore," Venice said.

And she was right. It was amazing.

"How much longer until everybody else arrives?" I asked.

"We have twenty minutes," Venice said.

And that really wasn't enough time. Seriously. Those minutes flew by. Everybody was trying to get everything perfect. Derby, in full Dracula gear, quickly strung more cobwebs near the beanbag toss. And members of the PTA set out strange-looking cupcakes that were so green they sort of glowed in the dark.

"Look at the photo booth!" Venice squealed.

It was so cool! It was shaped like a coffin. And inside was a little bench where two people could sit down. It looked like it was made out of bones.

"So adorable," I said. "Let's position the light here." I pointed to the exact spot where Venice was pointing. Sometimes it was like we shared the same brain.

When the costumes started rolling into the gym everything felt even more exciting. There was so much noise. And everybody was lining up to get a picture taken.

"You're doing such a great job," Ms. Kenny said. "Have you happened to see Javier and Anya?"

"No," Venice said. "They haven't helped with anything today."

And that was one of my favorite qualities about Venice. She just told it the way it was.

"You two are such a great team," Ms. Kenny said.

And it was almost like somebody had rung a bell signaling for Leo to show up. Because the second after that compliment, he trotted right over in his stupid helmet.

"Hey, Venice," Leo said, squeezing her hand. "Hey, Smudge."

I was sort of getting used to being called that.

"Are you sweating?" Venice asked him. "Maybe we should take our mining coats off. They are awful hot."

"I am sweating," he said. "But it's because I ran here."

That really bugged me. Because it was like he couldn't let Venice and me have one single lunch alone setting up for photos. He had to hurry his sweaty miner butt over here and interject himself as fast as he could.

"You're so sweet," Venice said.

"I didn't come for you," Leo said. "I came for Smudge."

"You don't need to call me that every second of your life," I said. I didn't mean to sound snarky, but it was so hard with him.

"I need to warn you," he said. "You're about to see something terrible."

"Leo," Venice said sharply. "That's not funny. Stop joking around."

"Brace yourself!" Leo said in a very panicked way. "It's ugly."

At first, I was really confused. What was I going to see? Was it really going to be *that* terrible? Probably Leo and I had different ideas about what was and wasn't terrible. But then it happened. And I was wrong. Leo and I did agree about what was terrible, and I was looking right at it. And he was completely right: It was ugly. It came out of the fog, or, more accurately, *they* did. Drea and Hayes. They were holding hands and smiling huge. They looked very happy to be a couple at the Big Boo. But that wasn't the terrible part. *Their costumes.* I couldn't believe my eyes.

"They should not be allowed to wear those!" Venice said. "It's wrong."

It was wrong. And hilarious. And mean. Drea and Hayes were dressed in all-black clothes with cut-up pieces of paper stuck to them. The papers had printed-out quotes on them. They were big. Everybody could read them. And they weren't quotes by dead presidents or famous writers. They were quotes from me! They were wearing my pops. And they weren't just wearing the pops I'd sent them. They'd also enlarged and printed out the few pops in my sewer. There they were. My pops. My username. My parents' pops. Their usernames. Drea and Hayes had dressed up as my PopRat account. And people loved it.

At first I felt like I was dying inside. I just wanted to fold up into myself a million times and then melt into the floor. Watching everybody approach those two and read the pops and then start laughing, it was too awful to see. I felt like all those laughers were misunderstanding who I was. Those pops were just something I shot out one morning without thinking very hard. I never expected them to be enlarged and turned into two Halloween costumes.

"Don't melt down," Venice said. "It's okay. Look at how much money you've raised for Smudge."

But it was pretty hard to feel anything other than humiliated. Because Drea and Hayes were mocking me. They had picked the most public place to tear me down, and then with a lot of paper and planning and stapling they'd struck out at me. They really did hate me. And they wanted to ruin my Halloween and more. From the looks of things, they were interested in destroying the rest of my life. Over a few dumb pops.

As they moved toward the photo booth, my embarrassment quickly turned to red-hot anger. It was hard for me not to hate them right back. Who did those two think they were? My pops didn't belong to them. It was hard for me to stand there and do my job and take pictures. It was hard for me to keep my cool and act like it didn't bother me that the two people approaching me were plastered in my own words. And guess what? As soon as they entered the coffin photo booth, I didn't keep my cool and stand right there and take it and do my job. No. Instead of taking their pictures, I, Perry Hall, snapped.

19

Quit It

The first sign that I had snapped was when I heard my own scream. I heard it escape my mouth and I could tell that it came from somewhere deep inside myself. Maybe my kidneys. Maybe even deeper. Then I felt myself charging toward them. Drea and Hayes looked really shocked at this. Their eyes were huge. As big as plates. As big as moons. And when I reached them, they probably thought I'd yell at them. I don't think they thought I'd lay a finger on them.

And technically, I didn't touch them. I touched my own property: my pops. I tore at their evil printouts. And I didn't feel bad about doing that at all. Those pops were mine. My words. My thoughts. And they belonged in my sewer, not stapled to two people who hated me. I yanked them off their shoulders, and stomachs, and knees. And did this yanking leave holes? Of course it did.

Those jerks had worn a cotton-spandex blend. As soon as I pulled the paper off, the staples cut through the fabric and revealed naked oval-shaped areas of skin, and maybe some underwear elastic. To be honest, I was ripping too fast and too hard to be certain of anything. I felt desperate. Drea was a geek who I'd been trying to help. We'd been in this together. And instead of being grateful, she'd invaded my life. She'd taken my sister's clothes and Hayes's crush on me and my pops. What was wrong with her? What made her think she could come to my house and eat my pizza and do this to me? It wasn't okay. No. I wasn't going to let Drea or Hayes parade around the Big Boo wearing my PopRat account. This was not happening.

And that was what I kept yelling, too. "This is not happening! This is not happening!"

Leo tried valiantly to hold me back. Even when I flung my arms to get away and accidentally knocked his miner's hat off and it slid across the gymnasium floor, nearly taking out a scarecrow. I kept diving at my pops. I felt like they belonged to me. And I wasn't going to leave Drea and Hayes alone until I had them all. Even Ms. Kenny couldn't stop me.

"Is this a planned stunt?" she asked.

"I wouldn't call it that," Venice replied.

It was when I saw Principal Hunt approaching that I knew I needed to stop ripping apart their terrible, awful PopRat costumes.

"It's not totally Perry's fault," Leo said loudly as Principal Hunt took stock of things.

"It's totally all Perry's fault!" Drea said. "She sent these pops. And once you send them they don't belong to you anymore. So I have every right in the world to wear them to this carnival."

"Pops?" Principal Hunt asked, looking back and forth between their partially shredded outfits and the pieces of paper I was clutching in my fists.

"Drea and Hayes are dressed as Perry's PopRat account. They're wearing all her personal pops," Venice explained.

"We got them out of her sewer," Hayes said. "Once they're in there it's public property, right? Isn't that how sewers work?"

"Venice, Leo, and Perry, please go to the library with Ms. Kenny," Principal Hunt said firmly. "I'll be there in five minutes."

Drea looked really happy when she heard this. But then the principal turned to her. "Drea and Hayes, in my office right now."

"But I don't want to miss Big Boo," Drea said. "I deserve to stay here."

"You should have thought of that before you picked such a hostile costume."

And I was sort of impressed that Drea had stood up for herself in this situation. Because I was the type of person who basically did whatever the principal told me to do.

"Head to the library," Ms. Kenny said. "I'm right behind you. I need to clean this up."

As the three of us walked back to the library, it was hard for me not to feel tremendously guilty for getting Venice kicked out of her first Big Boo.

"I'm sorry," I said. "I know I didn't handle that right. It just really hurt my feelings to see them dressed like that. Like what I'd said in my pops was a joke."

"It was harsh," Leo said. "I tried to warn you. But who ever thinks they're going to come face to face with all the crappy pops they've sent?"

I tried to ignore that Leo had called my pops crappy. I tried to focus on Venice.

"How mad are you, Venice?" I asked. I wanted to know where I stood with her.

"Well, I'm not as mad as you," she said. "It's crazy what you did back there."

We reached the library and she opened the door for me. I hung my head and entered. The librarian looked startled to see us.

"Aren't you missing the Big Boo?" she asked.

"We sure are," Leo said.

"Principal Hunt sent us here," Venice explained.

As soon as we sat down at a table, Ms. Kenny arrived.

"What a mess," she said, pulling up an undersized chair. "Okay. I need to know exactly how this started."

Everybody looked at me. Which surprised me. Because I had zero idea how things had gotten to this point. I pulled my fur paws off and stared at my hands.

"Are you and Drea frenemies?" Ms. Kenny asked me.

And it really bugged me that Drea was anything to me. She wasn't my friend. She wasn't my enemy. She was an annoying person who kept getting more annoying and so I tried to explain this to Ms. Kenny in a way that made me look sympathetic, and not like some angry costume attacker.

"I actually don't know her that well," I said. "One day, out of nowhere, she came to my house."

"That's not exactly right," Venice said. "You've known Drea for years."

"But just as a name. Not as a person. I didn't do stuff with her," I explained. "She was never my friend."

"What did she want when she came to your house?" Ms. Kenny asked.

And when I thought about that question, I realized how impossible Drea's request had been. "She wanted me to take a picture of her that was so awesome everybody would forget about the online clip of her throwing up all those hot dogs in a bucket at the fair."

"Doesn't she realize people stopped talking about that months ago?" Leo said. "It's old news."

"People still make puking sounds at her in the hallway," Venice said. "It's not *over* over."

"Did you agree to help her?" Ms. Kenny asked me.

And I tried hard to think of exactly what I'd said. But I couldn't totally remember. "I think I said I'd try."

Ms. Kenny exhaled and drummed her fingers on the table. "Venice and Leo, would you mind sitting over there and waiting for us?" She pointed to a table clear across the library.

"No problem," Leo said. He punched me in the shoulder as he left. Then he scooped up Venice's hand and they walked away.

It was all pretty awful. I felt like crying. But I didn't want to do that in front of Ms. Kenny.

"It's unfortunate what happened to Drea," Ms. Kenny said. "But you can't erase the Internet."

But I didn't think that was totally true. "Actually, stuff gets taken down all the time," I tried to explain.

"I know. But my point is that people have seen it and nobody can ever unsee something. Drea has to look ahead and move forward."

"Exactly," I said. "And a nice picture would have helped with that."

"Okay. So you agreed to take a nice picture. So then, how did these happen?" She spread the crumpled paper out on the table.

"Not those again," I whined, looking away.

"Perry, I like you. You're talented and an incredibly hard worker. And I do think you're nice. But you're also responsible for where you are here."

And it really sucked to hear Ms. Kenny say that.

"That's harsh," I mumbled. Because from where I was sitting I wasn't sure how I could've avoided all of it. Some of it, okay. But not *all* of it. I felt tears welling up in my eyes.

"Be careful what you take on," Ms. Kenny said. "Middle school should be fun. You should be spending time with your friends. Learning new things."

I glanced over at Venice. That seemed to be her middle school experience much more than mine.

"Is what I'm saying making sense?" Ms. Kenny asked, reaching out and squeezing my hand.

"Yeah," I said.

"I need to get back to the photo booth. I left Anya and Javier in charge and I need to check on them."

And then it sort of hit me. The complete unfairness of everything. The fact that I was crying in the library missing Big Boo because my attempts to help a geek look less geeky in the yearbook had totally backfired and the geek had ended up betraying me. And Anya was running the photo booth. How did she always come out on top? It felt like the world loved her more than it loved me. And that felt so wrong.

"Wait," I said as Ms. Kenny got up to leave. "I need to tell you something."

"Okay," she said. "Is it something you want me to pass along to Principal Hunt?"

I shrugged. "I want to quit."

"Quit?" Ms. Kenny looked surprised. "Quit what?"

"Yearbook," I said.

She let out a big breath. "Perry, you're too good to quit."

I shook my head again. "I think it's ruining my life. I eat, sleep, and drink tasks. Did you know I had thirty-seven of them?"

"Thirty-seven?" she asked, sounding surprised.

"Yes. I'm done. I can't keep doing this. Because I'm going to get suspended now, aren't I? Isn't that what happens when you attack students and put staple holes in their clothes? And then I'll fall super behind in my classes."

"I hope you don't get suspended," she said. She closed the space between us and gave me a hug. "I'm not going to let you quit right now. Come talk to me tomorrow. If you still feel the same way, we can transition you into something else."

And when she said it that way, that I could be transitioned into something else, my future felt a little scary. Because Yearbook had been the thing I'd wanted for so long. And now I had it. But it was killing me. So that meant it hadn't been the thing I'd really wanted, right? It had been the thing I thought I wanted when I thought it was something else.

I felt very confused that day when Ms. Kenny left the library. I had no idea what was going to happen to me. All I knew was that my parents were going to freak out when they learned about this. Which was probably happening at that very second.

20

Write My Name

Since I couldn't return to the Big Boo, my mom had to come pick me up at school. To say she was surprised, upset, and disappointed was an understatement. She arrived at the office in dust-covered workout clothes.

"You do your exercises in the garage now?" I asked, trying to avoid the subject of my punishment.

"I was moving heavy things," my mom said, standing in the doorway of the detention room, which was where Venice, Leo, and I were all being held until our moms came and got us. I had no idea what had happened to Drea and Hayes.

"Well, you look great," I said, picking up my backpack and walking toward the door.

"I just finished speaking to Principal Hunt. Your Pop-Rat account is history. And hand me your phone. You're grounded."

Giving her my phone made me feel very sad and very alone.

My mother continued her harsh tone with me all the way home. And when my dad got home, he was harsh too.

"You can't lunge at your classmates and destroy their clothes, no matter how offended you feel by their accessories," he said as we sat across from one another eating soy hot dogs on whole wheat buns.

"Right," I said. Because I figured that was the best thing to say.

"I blame Piper for some of this," my dad said, wagging his half-eaten hot dog at me. "She's unhinged the family. She's upset the order of everything."

But I felt like I needed to stand up for my sister. "I think hot dogs are more to blame for this than Piper."

My dad didn't understand Drea's history with that meat product, and that I was being serious.

"It's outrageous that you can joke about this. You've got detention again. You're the only Hall to ever get detention, and now you've had it twice."

"Your father's right," my mother said.

I started to tear up. "You think I want this?" I asked. "You think I wanted those kids to show up dressed like my PopRat account and have everybody laugh at me?"

My parents looked at each other and back at me.

"I know I've said this before, but I just don't remember middle school being this hard," my mom said.

"It's very, very hard," I said. Then I took a big drink of water and said what I'd been thinking all day. "I told Ms. Kenny I wanted to quit Yearbook."

My mom dabbed at her mouth with a paper napkin. "That's actually a worthwhile thing to consider."

My dad didn't look thrilled about this. "*Quit* is my least favorite verb."

"But I feel swallowed by it," I explained. "It's too much."

"Would Venice stay in it?" my mom asked.

I nodded. That made me so sad to admit. I hated the idea of leaving her there. We'd looked forward to that stupid class for months. But the reality was, it just wasn't an enjoyable elective.

"Does she know you want to quit?" my mom asked.

"Not yet," I said. My voice was breaking. "But she'll be fine. Her boyfriend is in there."

My mom and dad gave each other a glance.

"I think I'm going to go to my room," I said.

And I didn't even wait for my mom or dad to give me permission, I just took off. Once I was on my bed, it felt like my world was spinning. Was quitting the right thing? I wasn't sure. I probably wouldn't know for another month or so. After enough time had passed that I could decide whether I really missed it. While I was crying and feeling sorry for myself, my dad knocked gently on my door.

"Perry," he said sweetly. "Can I come in?"

"Actually," I called to him, "I need a few more minutes."

He knocked again. "You've got a phone call. It's Drea."

And that really blew my mind. She was the last person I wanted to speak with. "Tell her that she ruined my life and that I never want to take another call from her again."

He opened the door and came in. "Well, your mom has already talked to her mom and Drea wants to apologize, so I don't really feel like I can relay that message."

I flipped around. "But I don't want to talk to her, Dad."

"Just let her apologize. It's the civilized thing to do," he said.

That felt like a cheap excuse. Just because it was civilized didn't mean it would help anything get better faster. I dragged myself into the kitchen, and my mom handed me my phone. Then she kissed the top of my head.

"She sounds so sorry," my mom whispered.

Me: Hello?

Drea: I want you to know that I feel like total crap.

Me: Okay.

Drea: You were actually really helpful. My photos look great. And now I have a boyfriend. And I'm really happy.

Me: Um, my dad said you'd called me to apologize.

There was a long pause and I worried that she hadn't called to apologize at all. That she'd just called to brag about how great her life felt.

Drea: I took advantage of you. You said you'd help me fix my reputation. And instead of just taking what you could give, I got greedy. I wanted your sister's help too. And her clothes. And I knew it bugged you and I didn't care. It was crappy of me. I'm sorry.

I waited for her to mention dressing as my PopRat account. But she didn't say any more. I just listened to her breathing.

Me: Um, I'm still pretty upset that you dressed up as my PopRat account and tried to humiliate me at the Big Boo.

I could feel my parents staring at me.

Drea: You know, Hayes and I actually thought you'd find it funny. We didn't realize it would flip your switch. We were totally surprised when you leaped at us and tore off all the pops.

Was she being serious? It sounded like she was.

Me: Well, it was mean. Why would I find that funny?
Drea: We just didn't think it through. I didn't have a good idea for a costume. Neither did Hayes. And we were hanging out at his house, reading your pops over and over because we were both obsessed with how awful they made us feel. And then I said "Let's just wear them to school and call it a costume." And Hayes said, "Okay."

In the history of apologies, this one was pretty stinky. It was as if she didn't even understand what a lousy thing she'd done.

Me: You really hurt my feelings. And now I have detention.
Drea: Hayes and I have detention too. Principal Hunt was furious with us. She called us bullies. Can you believe that?
Me: Yes. I can.
Drea: Okay. You still sound pretty upset, so I'm going

to let you go. But I just want you to know that I know I
crossed a line. Hayes knows he did too. And we hope
you can stop hating us. We're sorry.

And here's the terrible truth about getting an apology.
Afterward, you have to accept it. Because if you don't, you stay
stuck in your own anger. Seriously. It will never go away.

I took a deep breath. "I don't hate you guys," I told her. "It
just created a bunch of drama I don't need."

"I feel you," Drea said. "And now I'm going to give you
what I should have given you a while ago: space. Bye!"

She hung up so fast I didn't even have time to say goodbye.
I clicked off my phone and set it on the table.

"Did it go okay?" my mom asked, gently rubbing my back.

"Drea Quan is a very intense nerd," I said. I felt a little off
balance after talking to her.

"Everybody needs to be happier and stress out less," my
dad said. "I think that's the takeaway here."

"And stop trying to help the nerds," my mom said. "It's
turning you into a different person. One who's in detention."

I nodded.

"I'm going back to my room," I said.

After I got there, I slipped into my softest pajamas and
climbed into my bed. My dad made it seem so easy: "Stress out
less and be happier." Could I do either of those things in Yearbook? I didn't know. All night long my mind ping-ponged the
idea of quitting. I couldn't quite imagine what my life would
feel like without it. What would I put in its place? What would
they do without me?

When I woke up I panicked a little bit, because I was going to be late for school. I rushed as fast as I could to get ready, and when I went to the table for breakfast, I asked a very logical question.

"Why didn't you wake me up?"

"You looked so peaceful," my mom said. "You never look like that anymore. I just couldn't bring myself to do it."

That answer bummed me out. Because it meant that any time I wasn't asleep my face looked disturbed.

As I nibbled on my toast, I asked another logical question: "How long until I get my phone back?"

Really, I thought my mom should have handed it over right then. What if Piper tried to text or call or pop?

"Your father took it to work with him," she said. "He's taking PopRat off it."

I didn't find that news too crushing. Though I was surprised he'd already left. "Did somebody break a tooth again?" I asked. Because Dad usually ate breakfast with us.

"They're thinking about hiring a third dentist," my mom said. "And if they do, we'll be seeing a lot more of your father."

I drank some orange juice and noticed a weird vase in the middle of the table.

"What is that thing?"

"It's not finished yet. Don't judge it," my mom said. "I still need to paint the tail feathers. And then I need to take it to Melinda's studio to get it fired and glazed."

I didn't know it had tail feathers. It looked very blobby.

"What kind of bird is it?" I asked. Because I didn't even know my mom liked birds.

"It's a turkey," she said. "I'm making a Thanksgiving centerpiece."

I couldn't even determine where its head was located.

"Huh," I said.

"You should come and pick out some greenware," my mom said. "They've got all kinds of fun stuff."

I stopped myself from complaining about not having enough time to start a ceramic project, because I realized that if I quit Yearbook I'd have loads of time.

"Maybe," I said.

My mom's face really lit up with that answer.

"I thought I'd drive you today," she said. "And I packed you a lunch for detention."

I let out a big depressing breath. "I should bring something to read too. It's rough in there."

When we opened the front door to leave I was surprised to see a box. It was from Drea. For one second, I was nervous that it was going to be something mean. Maybe her apology wasn't for real. Maybe she was just setting me up to really slam me.

Then my dad's advice popped into my head. "Stress out less and be happier." And so I decided to try that. I quickly pulled open the flaps and saw something amazing: all of Piper's clothes. It felt like this was where they belonged. The natural order of Piper's cute shirts should have been that after they finished living in Piper's closet, they came to live in mine. End of story.

When my mom pulled up to my school I sort of wanted to stay in the car. "Can't we go get doughnuts?" I asked.

"Running away from your problems doesn't solve your problems."

That comment hurt my feelings a little bit. Because I thought she was putting way too much emphasis on my problems.

"Go in there and have an awesome day!" My mom lifted up her hand to high-five me, which I really didn't feel like doing. But I went with the flow. She was trying really hard.

Walking into the school, I kept thinking everybody was looking at me. A few people definitely whispered when they saw me. I worried that they thought I was crazy. That I'd attacked Drea and Hayes for no reason. That I had anger issues. Or maybe some other issues. And I didn't want anybody thinking that. I wanted them to think of me as a normal person who took pictures.

Walking toward the Yearbook room, I felt my heart beating faster and faster inside my chest. Today was the day. I was either going to quit or stay. And there was no turning back. If I left, this was no longer going to be my classroom. If I left, I wasn't going to be building the yearbook this year or next. Because I was pretty sure Ms. Kenny wasn't going to admit a quitter for next year. I took the long way to class, and passed the drama room. The sign-up sheet for the school play was posted and there were a ton of names scribbled on it. I stopped to read it. It was so amazing to me that Derby had figured out a way to remake himself.

When school had started he was a zero. Now he was top dog in Drama. I knew Piper's magic wish hadn't made this happen—I knew magic was pretend—but it was really interesting to me that Derby had found his path, just like Piper had hoped. Then, before I could stop myself, I wrote my name down under the Tuesday tryout slot. Because why not? My schedule was really going to be opening up. I was going to need something to do with myself.

"Hey," a voice behind me said.

I flipped around. It was Leo. For a second I thought it was Hayes and I almost died. Because I just didn't know what to say to him.

"Bummer about detention," Leo said. "Totally unfair. I think you had a right to defend your pops."

And I sort of hated Leo in this moment. For bringing up my detention and my pops. It was like he was a cloud of terrible reminders. So I tried to say something helpful to him.

"You make my life sound awful," I said.

Then I left him and went to Yearbook. As soon as I walked into the room I felt really anxious. I spotted Venice and I headed straight for her, but Ms. Kenny stopped me.

"Meet me at the craft table," she said.

Venice glanced at me and mouthed, "You okay?"

I nodded. Not being able to talk or text with her made me feel like I was living in a box or in ancient times. It was lonely.

As I approached the craft table I saw something that surprised me. Tons of my photos were spread out on the table. Everything from the first assembly to the class clubs to the boys' volleyball team to the What's Hot portraits. I'd forgotten how many pictures I'd taken.

"You're a very talented workhorse," Ms. Kenny said.

I knew what she was doing. She was trying to convince me to stay. I felt so unsure about everything.

"I know you said you wanted to quit," Ms. Kenny went on. "And if that's truly what you want, I'm not going to talk you out of it. But I have an offer for you."

A teacher had never made me an offer before.

"What?" I asked.

"I want to de-task you," she said.

And that sounded too good to be true. "How will anything get done?"

"Just because you're good at everything doesn't mean that the burden should fall at your feet," Ms. Kenny said. "I'm limiting Javier's tasking duties. Students are allowed only three tasks a week."

That sounded too good to be true. I tried to understand how that would work. "What if I finish all three of my tasks by Wednesday? Do I get assigned three new tasks?" Because that was pretty easy math. That would mean I had six tasks. And chances were, under Javier's supervision, they would continue to inch higher and higher and multiply further.

"You can't get assigned new tasks until the following week," Ms. Kenny said.

I licked my lips. Then I chewed on them. That seemed so doable. I looked at Venice. She was working on portrait layout. I was going to miss her so much. Sure, we were in a couple of other classes together. But Yearbook was different. It was special.

"I'm not sure," I said. "I want to say yes, but I also want my life to feel simpler."

Ms. Kenny smiled at me. "Take a week. If you feel like quitting in a week, I'll help you transfer into a study hall."

Taking a week sounded like a reasonable thing to do. It was like a test period. If things still felt crappy, I could ditch this class. But if I was really starting to love it, then I could stay and keep having fun.

"What do you say?" she asked.

It was a pretty easy answer. "I like the idea of taking a week."

"Great!" Ms. Kenny said. "Why don't you go help Venice with layout. Maybe you can work on some captions. No stress."

And that all sounded fantastic.

"Leo," Ms. Kenny said, "bring Eli and Javier over. I have some questions about our sponsors."

And that was an amazing gesture, because it meant that Leo would leave Venice alone for the class instead of hover over and bug us.

Venice gave me a quick hug when I joined her. "I knew you wouldn't quit. You'd never leave me. I'd never leave you. It's just how we're made."

"Actually," I said, "I only agreed to stay a week. And I'll see how I feel then. I might still quit."

Venice's face fell in total disappointment. So I gave her some advice. "Stress less and be happier. Maybe I'll stay."

"Okay," she said. "Look at how awesome these portraits look."

And it was hard to deny that they looked really amazing. Everybody's eyes were open and looked bright and natural.

"You've done so much for the nerds," Venice said. "Really."

I was glad Venice felt that way. But I wasn't totally sure. I felt like I'd done all I could do as far as Yearbook was concerned. But I wasn't sure if it was enough. If the unpopular kids wanted to change the system and become more popular, they needed to do it without me. Just like Derby. They needed to find their own paths.

21

Fried

I woke to the sound of somebody in my closet.

"Mitten Man, get out!" I scolded. I had never understood his desire to scratch at the back of my closet during predawn hours.

"Shhh, Perry. You'll wake Mom and Dad."

Piper. I bolted upright. I couldn't believe she was here. In my room. With me. Was I dreaming? I pinched myself. Ouch. I was not dreaming.

"Why are you here?" I asked.

"I called Drea and she said she gave you my clothes and I need them back," she said.

"For Thailand?" I'd started to accept the fact that Piper was old enough to do what she wanted. Even if it meant leaving me.

"Okay," she said. "If I tell you something, will you promise not to tell Mom and Dad?" She sat down on the end of my bed and squeezed my foot underneath the covers.

"Probably," I said.

Piper let go of my foot and frowned. "That's a pretty worthless promise."

I sat up straighter. "Just tell me."

She exhaled dramatically and ran her hands through her hair. "They'll find out soon enough anyway. Okay. Are you ready?"

I swatted her with my pillow. "Spill it."

"I dumped Bobby," she said.

She had a big smile on her face when she said this, which didn't make any sense to me. Because I had figured if those two ever called it quits she'd be sad for a century. I tried to uncover more details.

"What happened? I thought you loved Bobby."

"I know. Okay. Remember how upset I got with you guys for not changing when I was changing?" she asked.

I totally remembered that fight. Because it happened the day she made us throw away all our good food.

"So I realized that Bobby was the real problem. He was rigid and I'm super flex. It was impossible for us to stay together and for me to stay my own person. It's like he wanted me to become a female Bobby. He wanted to date himself."

That sounded horrible. "Well, I'm really glad you stayed your own person." I couldn't picture Piper as anybody else. And I especially couldn't picture her as a female Bobby.

The door to my room squeaked open and my mom stood there with crazy hair.

"I am not giving you your passport," she said, angrily pointing her finger at Piper.

For some reason, this made Piper laugh uncontrollably.

My dad appeared in my doorway, and his hair looked even crazier. "I am standing with your mother on this."

Piper stopped laughing and went to them and gave them hugs. "Yeah. I took my passport weeks ago. Bobby gave me his dead aunt Bev's passport and I put it in your file cabinet. I can't believe you never checked the picture."

My mother looked horrified.

"Don't worry," I said. "She's not going. She dumped Bobby."

Piper rolled her eyes. "You didn't even try to keep that a secret."

"Good news should never be a secret," I said.

"By the way," Piper said, "I'm totally eating crap food again. I actually brought vegetable oil and a bowl of dough. I figured we can make Utah scones. Did we keep the honey?"

I smiled huge when she said that. Because we did keep the honey.

"You guys look traumatized," Piper said, pointing to my parents.

"It's been a big week," my mother said.

"We're not ever having another week like that again," my father said.

But I was just so happy with my morning. It was one of the best I'd had in a long time. My mom and dad sat down on my bed with me and Piper. Eventually Mitten Man wound his way into the mix too. And it felt so good to be hanging out and laughing as a family. My mom. My dad. Piper. I was so happy to have them all.

It was a perfect moment. Until I heard the worst sound in the world coming out of my mom's bathrobe pocket. "Stressed

Out" by Twenty-One Pilots. It could only mean one thing: Hayes was calling me. I stopped breathing. My mom lifted up my phone to see who it was.

"I love that song," Piper said, humming along.

"Okay," I said, sounding very serious. "Whatever we do, we cannot answer that call."

"Hello?" my mother said, answering the call. Which really stunned me. Just because I was grounded and had lost full use of my phone didn't give her the right to answer all my incoming calls. Did it?

"Stop looking so freaked out," Piper said. "You're killing the mood."

While I bet that was true, it was impossible for me to stop looking and feeling horrified. Why would Hayes be calling me? What could he possibly have to say to me that couldn't wait for a few months or possibly years?

"Yes," my mother said. "She is here, but she's grounded."

My father rubbed my shoulder. "This is the third or fourth time he's tried to call. It's the boy who dressed up in your text messages, right?"

"Pops," I mumbled. "He stapled my pops to himself."

"Ouch," Piper said. "He did *what*?"

But I didn't have time to explain the Big Boo drama to Piper, because before I could even process what was happening, my mom had handed me back my phone and I was listening to Hayes talk to me.

Hayes: Perry, I want you to know that I feel rotten. Like, worse than a dog.

Silence.

Hayes: Perry? Are you there?
Me: Yeah.
Hayes: What I did to you is probably the crappiest thing
    I've done in my whole life. I'm not sure why I did it. I
    can't explain it. Your pops turned me into a different
    person.
Me: Um, I probably shouldn't have sent them.

Then I heard some shuffling sounds, like maybe Hayes
had dropped his phone.

Hayes: What did you just say?
Me: I said that I probably shouldn't have sent them.

It was totally awkward talking to Hayes. My mouth felt
really dry and my entire family was in the room with me.

Hayes: Wow. You mean that?
Me: Uh, yeah. I think so.

"Is he apologizing to you?" my mother asked. "He said that
he needed to make things right. He sounded sincerely upset."
I nodded and plugged my finger into my other ear. I
needed to focus on Hayes, not my mom.

Hayes: Okay. Now I don't feel totally weird about telling
    you this.

He might not have felt weird, but I did.

Hayes: I left something for you in your mailbox. That's it.
  Bye!
Me: Hayes? Are you there? Hello?

"If you're done talking, I need your phone back," my mom said, reaching out to take it. "You're still grounded."

"Perry is grounded again?" Piper said, flopping back on my pillows. "You barely got ungrounded."

"I got detention again too," I said, joining Piper by my pillows. "But now that I know the ropes, I'm less freaked out about it."

"Getting desensitized to detention is not a good thing," my dad said sternly.

He looked so tired standing next to my floor lamp in his giraffe-spotted bathrobe. Life was so unpredictable. Last Christmas, when I picked out that bathrobe for him at JCPenney, I had no idea he'd be lecturing me in it about my second round of detention.

"I really don't want to talk about any of this. I just want to eat scones and enjoy Piper and feel as happy as I did ten minutes ago," I said.

"Sounds good to me," my mother said, smoothing her crazy bed head.

"Let's get in the kitchen and heat up the oil," my dad said. "The scones aren't going to deep-fry themselves."

As I was trying to figure out a way to sneak out to the mailbox, I felt Piper put an arm around me.

"I know what's in the mailbox," she whispered to me.

How was that possible? But instead of asking her, I just stared at her in disbelief.

"Close your mouth," Piper said. "He left this for you." She slipped an envelope into my hands.

So then I asked the obvious question. "Why did you take my mail?" Between my mom answering my phone calls and Piper intercepting my private letters, my life felt very violated.

"I did you a favor!" Piper said. "Did you want Mom to find that? Or Dad? If this kid really likes you, you have no idea what could be in there."

Piper swiped a pot of my huckleberry lip balm from my dresser and took off the lid. It bothered me that she didn't ask for permission to use it before she slathered it on her lips.

"I think I'm dehydrated," she said. "My skin feels so dry."

I could feel my eyes bugging out. How could Piper be talking about her skin moisture levels at a time like this?

"Where should I hide it?" I asked. Because I definitely felt way too scared to read that letter. It could say anything. *Anything.*

"What are you talking about? You need to stay here and read it. Compose yourself. And then come out and eat scones with us and act totally normal. Okay?"

Okay? Things felt very far away from being okay. The letter felt radioactive in my hands. I didn't want to read it. It was the last thing in the world I wanted to do.

"I'll open it later," I said.

"Dumb move," Piper said. "I drive back to Pocatello this afternoon. You're probably going to need my guidance."

I sighed. I probably would. Boy issues weren't anything I'd

had to deal with before. Trying to solve this problem alone felt like a disastrous move.

"I'll keep Mom and Dad busy. It's best to tackle your problems right away. Quit trying to run from them."

But that felt like an unfair thing to say. Because I didn't even know I had this problem until two minutes ago. Piper hurried down the hall and began chatting loudly with our dad about a high-pressure weather system that was bringing a heavy rainstorm into the area. My dad loved talking about the jet stream and storm fronts. If he weren't a dentist, I could imagine him being a meteorologist.

I slowly closed my bedroom door and sat on my bed. My hands were shaking. Hayes had written my name in tiny letters across the front. *Perry.* I flipped it over and broke open the envelope's flap with my thumb. The paper inside looked fancy. It had tiny evergreen trees printed along its top edge. I took a deep breath. And I read what Hayes had written.

Perry, you're wrong. You don't know anything about crushes.

My stomach flipped with excitement. Why had my stomach done that? I didn't like Hayes, did I? What did this note even mean? Did Hayes still like me? And if he did, did that also mean he didn't like Drea? Wasn't he Drea's boyfriend? Weren't they official? If somebody else's official boyfriend leaves a letter like this in your mailbox, does it mean he's a terrible person? Does it mean I'm a terrible person? Or does it mean something else entirely?

I thought of Hayes in his orange T-shirt. PERSEVERE. Maybe his crush wasn't going anywhere.

"Perry!" my mother called. "We're debating whether or not to put chocolate chips in the scones. We need you."

"Coming," I called. But I thought the answer to that question was obvious. Chocolate chips go with anything. Even a cup of ice.

I folded up the letter and stuffed it under my mattress. I'd never hidden anything under my mattress before. But I'd never gotten a letter from a boy like this before either.

Middle school. It was a giant, never-ending roller-coaster ride of things I never expected to happen. And for some inexplicable reason, knowing this was how it worked, and not knowing how it was going to turn out, made my stomach flip with excitement one more time.

Acknowledgments

First, I must thank my agent, Sara Crowe, who has sold a dozen novels for me and has helped steer my life toward a place of abundance and happiness, even though it never feels that way during the drafting process. I want to thank my husband, Brian Evenson, who is always willing to lend his writerly talents to anything I'm writing, even grocery lists. And our son, Max, whose interest in dinosaurs and wild boars will most likely creep into my work. My Alcatraz gardening friends have remained present and supportive, even though I'm now far away from the island. I miss you all, especially Kristin Scheel, Tracy Roberts, and Shelagh Fritz. Writer friends always lift me, and that includes Claudia Rankine, Kathryn Davis, Eric Zencey, Maria Finn, and my Rhode Island writing group: Kara LaReau, Anika Denise, and Jamie Michalak. As with the first book, Hanna Jones provides good inspiration. And special thanks to my sister, Julie, and my nieces and nephews for keeping me close to my Idaho roots. Same goes for Mom, Dad, and Doreen. And most importantly, I want to thank my fabulous editor, Wendy Loggia, who never fails to make my work funnier, brighter, and more true. This is the sixth novel she's shepherded into the world, and they are what they are because of her. If there is such thing as an editor lottery, I won it.

About the Author

KRISTEN TRACY is the author of many popular novels. She lives with her family in the popular state of California. Visit her at kristentracy.com (it will make her feel popular).

Make sure to read the first
PROJECT [UN]POPULAR book!

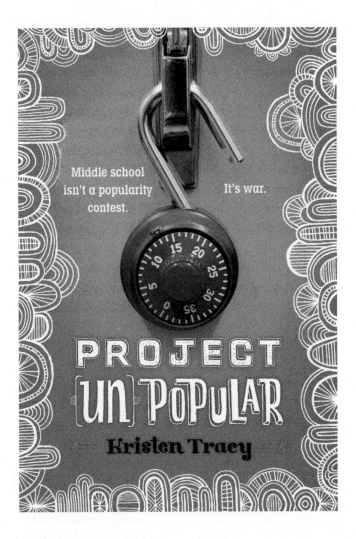